Beyond Tomorrow

IAN LUMLEY

Published by Ian Lumley
Publishing partner: Paragon Publishing, Rothersthorpe
First published 2017
© Ian Lumley 2017

ISBN 978-1-78222-505-8

Book design, layout and production management by Into Print
www.intoprint.net
01604 832149

Printed and bound in UK and USA by Lightning Source

ACKNOWLEDGEMENTS

Grateful thanks are due to:

Ian Russell for his Gaelic, and for his patience in answering
my many questions at the most inconvenient times. His
forbearance is acknowledged and appreciated.
Myra Christie for her review of the text and professional
editing efforts.
Ann, for her continuing and continuous support; the cover
picture; her proof reading; and her ability to shed the light of
realism on my sometimes wilder thoughts!

To three special boys:

Joshua, Oliver and Theodore

1.

THE FORSTER CHIP, initially developed over twenty years ago, had been created as part of the research into Alzheimer's disease and the subsequent onset of Dementia which was a common pathway for the disease to develop, especially amongst the elderly. These illnesses, primarily but not exclusively of old age, frequently removed the ability to communicate with any degree of clarity, and so clinicians had worked 'in the dark' for a number of years trying to discern what a patient's actual symptoms were for those suffering from such ailments. What they felt and where, had (until the discovery of the chip) been largely a matter of guesswork for those trying to help.

Benjamin Forster's discovery changed all that. The nano impulses it sent out into the brain, once successfully implanted there, were able to establish not only the extent of any damage to the neural pathways, but also to report these back wirelessly to the Consultants waiting 'outside'. The coming together of micro technology and medicine was not new. It had started over fifty years earlier with such now mundane activities as so called 'keyhole' surgery. The nano chip, however, took this technology to completely different levels. Not only did it take miniaturisation to a completely new degree of sophistication, it also enabled the creation of links to the neural network and pathways within the brain structure itself. Once implanted, over a period of several months, it began to work as if it were part of the brain function itself. It took time, but when this was married to the new ability to send wireless messages back to the computer tablets that all medical staff now carried as a matter of course, what some clinicians were already beginning to call a new branch of science, began to show real promise – and not only in the original areas that had led to its development.

A software package (named rather incongruously 'Dementapp') was quickly developed that could translate the electronic impulses into signals which showed a very strong correlation to the normal synaptic responses received from different parts of the brain structure of patients with no trace of the disease. It quickly became apparent that what the medical staff were looking at was a totally new and very powerful tool. This new technology was swiftly tried against some of the more severely affected patients suffering from Alzheimer's and Dementia. The results which were now coming from those early attempts were so promising that it was clear that dramatic improvements in the treatment of this disease were on the horizon.

It didn't take long for the minds involved in this new frontier of science to see that with just a little modification here and there, there was a real possibility of introducing a two-way path for transport of information that would allow changes to the brain functions at the molecular level to be made. Assessment of the patients response to stimuli and comparison against 'normal' individuals as shown in several small trials, led to new 'instructions' being fed down the line and when, taken up by the affected brain, caused a significant lessening of the symptoms. Some patients were now able to function near to the norm, where before they had been approaching some kind of catatonic stage in their disease. Even before this two-way communication process had been fully assessed, it was apparent that behaviours of the most severely affected patients could be markedly improved.

Regulatory bodies responsible for the evaluation of 'new' technologies in the medical sphere were notorious for their conservative approach to the release of new drugs and treatments into the system, recognising some of the errors of the past, such as Thalidomide. The success of these new efforts was such, however, that they were being put under great pressure to allow them to be fast tracked into general use. The ever-increasing number of people suffering from such complaints and the ever present TV documentaries which dwelt on the failure to provide anything approaching a worthwhile cure, played their part in that pressure.

Within a very short space of time, they had decided that, in spite of the reservations some of the senior clinicians still held about the secondary affects of this new treatment, more emphasis on this research was vital. They also decided that confidential discussions with firms who might be able to develop this new technology and bring it into the public domain, should begin as soon as possible.

2.

HILARY WATSON HAD always known she was destined for great things – to be the best of the best. Being born on the first morning of the new Millennium had been a sure signal of that destiny. Throughout her schooling at Malvern Girls College and then Oxford, she had attained that distinction. Of course her family's farming roots in the Worcestershire countryside had given her the silver spoon so often talked about by others – behind her back. She knew of the envy, and had not allowed it to deflect her from her aims – to rise above petty jealousies and achieve things on her own merits.

A short, but very successful career – one of her senior Law Partners had actually described her performance as 'stellar' – at the Bar, had followed where she had specialised in Immigration issues. Seen by many as the most able QC to have come along in some time, she had been assessed in one of her early appraisals by her senior mentor in the following terms:

'She argues as though she is fighting for her life, regardless of the position she has to take' and 'A very solid advocate, she is clear-thinking, methodical and pulls no punches.'

Men had never played an important part in her life. Her father had been a largely absentee landlord for the tenants of the variety of farms he owned in the Worcestershire Countryside, and he was an absentee father too, for much of the time.

She had only had one relationship of note. She had met Geoffrey Williams at one of the innumerable Oxford parties she had attended in an effort to be seen as 'one of the girls'. There had been the beginnings of an attraction there, she would not deny that, but it had never really got off the ground, because he had graduated and moved away while she was still in the middle of her own studies. She learned later that he had gone into the Cambridge backwaters when he took up a position in one of the Scientific Research Units – something to do with GPS, she seemed to remember. It hadn't unduly bothered her then, and it didn't unduly bother her now. She had been far too busy carving out her own career to be sidetracked by something as frivolous as a 'relationship'.

It was no surprise to anyone who had come into contact with her in those earlier days that she was quickly head-hunted for the safe Hampshire Conservative Parliamentary seat based in Winchester. When she had entered Parliament at the next election she quickly impressed even those who did not share her somewhat extreme right wing views.

After a spell working to the Justice Secretary, she had been elevated to the Home Office hot-seat after the last election. Frank Sutherland, as the Prime Minister, had watched her almost meteoric rise and felt she would be eminently suited to this big role within his second Government. She was determined to prove him right, but not at the expense of modifying her own beliefs on how the British people should be handled.

She felt no particular loyalty to Sutherland. In fact, if the truth be known, she thought him a rather typical male wimp. She did not need to be told that most of the allegiances and alliances which were forged in Westminster rarely lasted as long as it took the ink to dry on a document. She was not disposed anyway to tie her flag to someone else's mast. She was much more concerned with fashioning her own.

She had decided when she became a Member of Parliament that she should buy a home somewhere in the Constituency. Living outside the Constituency boundaries had given rise to questions on the credibility and even – in one case – the loyalty of other Members of Parliament and she had no desire to have anyone making life more difficult for her than need be. She had realised from the outset, however, that her days in Westminster would mean that she would need someone to look after the house she had eventually bought in Blackberry Lane on the edge of the village of Four Marks to the north of Hampshire.

Sally Thomas, a native of South Wales, who lived in the village with her partner, Walter Hughes, had seemed like a good choice for that role when she had advertised the position, and so it had turned out. When the Home Office position came along, it was clear that Hilary could not undertake the increased responsibilities from her home 'out in the sticks'. Getting home would only be possible, she knew, at weekends and even then there would be the inevitable 'surgeries' to allow her new found constituents to make representations to her about their concerns. As a result she made arrangements to lease a flat nearer to Westminster.

Following a short discussion between the two women, it was agreed that Sally would increase the hours she already devoted to the Hampshire house, becoming a quasi secretary, in Hilary's absence. Walter, who was in the market garden business anyway, would also look after the garden in her absence.

While those arrangements were being agreed, a team of security experts from MI5 came in to look the new home over. Their responsibility, the leader had said, was to identify any security issues for Hilary, now that she was occupying one of the most senior positions in the Cabinet. She was quite happy with his suggestions for increased lighting around the property, and the almost inevitable security cameras were fitted up and working in a matter of days. She was less enthusiastic about the proposal to install 'panic' buttons in every room in the house. She even laughed outright when he suggested that two should be installed in her en-suite.

'Why on Earth would I want to do that?' she enquired.

'Terrorists do not always come at the most convenient time Mam' he replied. 'If you were in the bath, or even sitting over there – he gestured to the toilet – when they decided to pay a visit, you would not have time to reach a button in the bedroom, would you?'

She still felt that it would be a waste of money, but

when he made it clear that he was not going to 'sign off' the premises to say they were secure unless she agreed, she gave in. She had a feeling that Frank Sutherland would not thank her for creating a stir about the Home Secretary rejecting security advice from her own experts.

Sally Thomas, for her part, was quite pleased to be asked to increase her role for Hilary. She sometimes wondered what her ex-husband Bryn back in South Wales would say if he knew the circles she now moved in. Being part of the great and the good had always had an attraction for him. That had always been denied him, and she almost felt sorry for him that he could never seem to see that it was his own attitudes and approach to people which had left him short of the importance he had so obviously craved. Then she remembered the eternal rows and some of the things that had been said, and she wasn't sorry any longer.

3.

EILEAN LEÒDHAIS – MORE commonly known as The Isle of Lewis – was the largest and most northerly of the group of Islands known to everyone as the Outer Hebrides. Placed as it was some 50 miles west of the mainland of Scotland, it was far enough away to retain it's own character and not be influenced by the excesses of the rest of the country. At least that is what a variety of Ministers in Stornoway would preach from the pulpit of their church on a Sunday morning. It was one of the few things that they all agreed on. For an Island community of less than twenty thousand souls in total, it boasted no less than nine different religious denominations active within its borders – mainly in the only town of any size, Stornoway.

Donald McLeod had lived most of his life among the largely flat landscape that was the Isle of Lewis. Unlike so many of their erstwhile school friends, he and his younger brother Colin had never shown any desire to seek their fame and fortune elsewhere. Yes, the surrounding countryside was flat and largely uninteresting – especially in the northern part where they, along with most of the Island population, had their home. Yes, the climate took a bit of getting used to. Temperatures never rose much above sixty degrees even in the height of summer and never dropped much below fifty even in what to the islanders was the depths of winter. The surrounding sea saw to that. However, many of the Islanders took a perverse pleasure in being known as 'hardy' and 'self sufficient'. The Island way of life certainly taught them that the best person to rely on when things went awry was themselves. Apart from the town of Stornoway itself, there were often many miles between neighbours who live on the further edges of the land looking out across the Atlantic as it brought in ocean swells which had often started on the East Coast of America.

Donald and his brother, however, had always felt comfortable amongst their 'ain folk' and had no desire to travel further afield to find fulfillment in their lives. Colin had developed a love of language early in his own life. A voracious reader, he was more often to be found sitting on a bench at the side of the local rugby pitch engrossed in his latest book acquisition, rather than playing in the middle of the park. It was no surprise to anyone when he eventually announced that he was leaving the Island to get a degree in Gaelic. There were several Universities who provided courses that would fit the needs of the young student, but he discovered, much to his own surprise, that the University with the best record of success at final examination time was Edinburgh rather than the more obvious one based in Dingwall called The University of The Highlands and Islands (UHI). It was with a certain amount of trepidation therefore that he had set out for the faraway Capital of Scotland, making clear his desire to return and find work on the Island as soon as he had finished his studies.

Donald, the elder by a mere two years, was entranced by the stories he had heard repeated at his local Sunday School. The idea of gaining salvation from the sins of the world expounded there had a profound effect on the young Christian. The story of Jesus casting moneylenders out of the temple found a ready audience with him. He had seen some of the things that went on just under the surface of the Island community and knew that there was a vital role for someone to cast out latter day demons from amongst the otherwise God fearing people. He saw a role for himself in that and resolved to be a different animal to the sometimes mealy mouthed mutterings he had heard from visiting members of the clergy. He had not yet heard the term 'Fire and Brimstone' but he already knew what it meant, and was attracted to it.

Long before he finished his schooling on the Island he had a clear idea of what the future – his future – was to be. Unlike his younger brother, however, he had no intention of travelling far from home to get his qualifications. UHI would do just fine for the budding member of the clergy. There he would get the background education to marry to his personal delivery of *THE WORD*. Like his brother, he fully intended to return to Stornoway and begin his Evangelical efforts amongst his own people. There, he knew, they would understand his approach, or they would soon learn!

During the course of those studies he had to undertake three separate 'placements' to allow him to gain practical experience of a hands-on role in the Ministry. These also allowed others than his own course tutors to assess the worth – and failings – of the prospective clergyman, before he was let loose on an unsuspecting parish. The first of these was with Kiltearn Parish Church set in the small village of Evanton on the shores of the Cromarty Firth. There he found a ministry which typified the small community it served. No threat of damnation here, merely a gentleness of spirit and an even more gentle approach to any waywardness from the teachings in the Bible.

Donald had a great deal of difficulty in keeping quiet when he saw some of the work being done by the elderly Minister in charge. He knew however that, no matter his own views, those of this man would carry a great deal of weight at the University when the eventual assessment of his own work reached them later. He decided early on in that placement that silence would, in this case, be close to golden. The experience, however, only strengthened his own belief that not only was there another way to carry the word of God to others, but that it was a better way.

When his third and final placement was discussed, he was ecstatic when he discovered that it was to be back on his beloved Island. There he was to serve with the Parish of Martin's Memorial Church. This was one of the largest congregations on the Island, and the Minister, one Murdo MacDonald, came from the Islands himself – in his case Tiree.

There, in the hamlet of Scarinish, Murdo had been raised in surroundings he described as next door to Heaven. A necklace of little bays sheltered from the fierce North Atlantic storms with only a smattering of houses and the inevitable sheep, meant that he had been sheltered not only from the worst of the weather as he grew up, but also any knowledge of man's capacity for evil. He saw Stornoway and his charge on Francis Street as a huge Metropolis and, Donald recognised, so it must have seemed to a man brought up in such isolation. Donald could also see that it was a charge that the man was just not capable of handling.

Donald was put in something of a quandary. He liked Murdo as a man, recognising the good that was in him, but he also felt the need to do something that would shake him and his congregation out of the rut they were clearly in. When he had raised at one of the early session meetings that he was concerned at the fact that membership of the Church had fallen to its lowest level for nearly twenty years, he was dismayed at the response. None of the elders said anything, but then they rarely did, preferring to wait until the Minister had spoken and then falling in line with whatever he said. Murdo had said that he felt it was wise to concentrate on the quality of the membership rather than dwell on numbers alone. As the others nodded their heads in agreement with this pronouncement, Donald knew he had to do something, and soon.

What that something might be, he never found out. A sudden heart attack and an even more sudden burial meant that he would never get the chance for what would undoubtedly have been a difficult conversation with Murdo. At Murdo's funeral, the Clerk to the Lewis Presbytery took Donald to one side and said

'we would like you to remain here in temporary charge until we have had a chance to discuss the future for Martin's at our next meeting. Murdo has spoken highly of you in his interim report on your placement and he clearly felt that you could handle the responsibility.' Donald was glad to accept that role.

Some six months later he was asked if he would contemplate taking the charge forward permanently. So it was that Donald McLeod became the newest and youngest Church Of Scotland Minister in the history of the Lewis Presbytery.

4.

FRANK SUTHERLAND HAD come into Parliament as part of the huge reactionary movement which had characterised the 2019 election. He remembered with some glee how one reporter had written at the time 'how can the British public be expected to make an informed decision between the parties when they are all pursuing reactionary policies?' Well they could, and they did.

The difference was, of course, that the rump of the 'old' Labour Party wanted to take the Country back to Victorian times when policies such as nationalisation had been such a big vote winner. That long ago decision by the Indians to close the last centre for steelmaking in the UK at Port Talbot in South Wales, had been their final undoing. The Labour Party had always prided itself on being a 'broad church'. That essentially allowed a wide scope of views to be fully considered before they took a united view on the way to deal with anything. It didn't mean, however, that the eventual view reached was any better, just that it had taken a far longer time to get there. It was Clement Attlee who had once said 'Democracy means government by discussion, but it is only effective if you can stop people talking.'

Trying to get that plant renationalised was a step too far back in time for most people. When that didn't happen, the 'broad church' that they lauded so much had quickly descended into a bitter feud between the different factions. They had spent so much time arguing with each other that they eventually became irrelevant to the vast majority of the British people. Their hopes of getting back into Government had died along with those arguments.

He did not need reminding how close the Conservative Party had come to blowing that opportunity. Theresa May, the Prime Minister of the day, had been a fervent follower of the Thatcher policies which had emerged as far back as the 1980s. This had meant that successive Governments had overseen the sale of a wide variety of British assets to anyone who paid the most money – all under the sacred tenet of 'rolling back the state'. There had never been much of a problem when this approach was concentrating on the sale of private companies, but it had come as a something of a shock to many people to realise that the electrical and water infrastructure of the country was now almost completely under the ownership of either the French or the Germans. How the public might have reacted if, instead of the Indians closing a steel making plant in South Wales, water or electrical supplies were to be dramatically cut back in the South of England, was likely to have been seen in quite a different light.

If the Labour Party had not been so stuck in the 1930s, they might have been able to draw a closer connection between what the Indians were doing then and what the French and Germans might do in the future. In that case, they might well have been elected, and the course of British political history over the next quarter of a century would have been vastly different, he mused.

The Conservative Party – he smiled at the thought that it was 'his' Conservative Party now – on the other hand, had wanted to take a step back from the EU immigration policies which had forced Great Britain to take large numbers of immigrants fleeing from the fighting in the Middle East. The economic affect in terms of job opportunities for our own population as well as depressing the wages on offer, of so many arriving on our shores desperate for work, was bad enough. But it had become clear very early on that some (far too many) of those immigrants were, in fact, religious terrorists who were able to use the increasing migration flow northwards as an easy way of coming to this country, and others, before venting their acts of terror against the local populace. He reminded himself that that was one concern which had raised its head again recently.

This time the influx was coming, mainly by sea up through the Bay of Biscay, from the shores of Africa, but the problems it was creating were no different to the previous ones. He knew he needed to find a quick solution to that one, or it might get out of hand, rather as the last one had. Troops on the street, for whatever reason, is never the sign of a Government in control of a situation.

The prison population had risen quite sharply as a

succession of criminal cases had put large numbers of so-called Illegal Immigrants behind bars for their actions when they came to these shores. Of course being in Europe had meant that the Court of Human Rights had then got involved in hearing interminable complaints from 'ambulance chasing' lawyers about the rights of these terrorists not to be sent home again. In one celebrated case a Somali citizen who had arrived in England illegally and then proceeded to commit several criminal acts against children and others, was allowed to stay here because the Somali Government refused to accept him back as he was being 'forced into deportation'. The European Court had ruled, much to the derision of nearly every Country in the EU, that it would infringe his 'human rights' to send him back – to his own Country!

Frank could never say it out loud to anyone, of course, but it had been one occasion where the prison population had demonstrated that there is still some form of justice not bound by European Legislation, no matter how roughly it may be meted out. The Somali had eventually pleaded to be allowed to return to his birthplace rather than suffer more at the hands of the other inmates.

That particular type of fiasco was still in progress, even after all these years. The time taken to get even a small number of cases through the legal system was painfully long to say the least. Of course, the cost of keeping these people banged up while this was going on was an ever increasing burden on the British taxpayer, but he knew he would get nowhere with that argument when it was human rights that were being discussed.

Nevertheless, something had to be done about the situation. The latest news about the possibility of another large influx of immigrants was going to be the straw that broke the camel's back, both in financial and political terms. He had no doubt that, if solutions were not found – and soon – it was more than likely to do great damage to his party's chances at the next General Election scheduled for three years from now.

His party had, however, touched on a collective nerve in the British psyche when it said that they had to be more in control of matters which affected their ability to have a stable society. In particular, they had to be able to control who came into their own country, and what those individuals did afterwards. Ever since the long off days when Ted Heath had tried desperately, and eventually successfully, to get Britain accepted into the burgeoning European Union, many in his party had been ambivalent about the consequences of such a move.

He remembered only too well that old war horse, Enoch Powell, railing against the loss of sovereignty which he foresaw as an inevitable consequence of joining our 'partners' in Europe. Frank himself, and now an increasing number of his party, had come around to the same view. At the time, of course, the memories of Powell's 'rivers of blood' speech was just too fresh, and too violent, for most of the party to take on board. By the time 2019 came along however, millions of voters, including many erstwhile Labour Party die-hards, had agreed that enough was enough.

That election had seen the end of the Labour Party as a force in British politics. The former Liberal Democrats were still, all these years later, trying to find a middle ground that they could call their own and build some kind of following. His biggest problem as he saw it, as the new leader and now Prime Minister, was in trying to prevent an even more pronounced lurch to the right from a group of MPs who felt they had no real opposition in the house, or elsewhere. That attitude had been the downfall of many a politician before, and he was determined it would not happen to him.

The meeting he was just getting ready for today was with three of his Cabinet colleagues and would bring him up against two of the major players who felt that way. The Minsters at the Foreign Office and the Home Office were both what had used to be termed 'Hawks'.

Hilary Watson at the Home Office was one of those women – people he thought, dammit. People. He had to watch his tongue. He knew that you couldn't say *women* like that nowadays; otherwise some bright spark would accuse him of being sexist, wouldn't they? Anyway she was one of those *people* who seemed to have been brought up in a very different world to his. She seemed to lack what used to be called the milk of human kindness. In fact, she seemed to be completely devoid of any emotions at all. As one of the brightest of QC's before she had entered Parliament, her training had made her see everything in adversarial terms.

If he was honest, it was one of the qualities which had made her seem well fitted to the role she now enjoyed. The Home Office was one of the largest Departments in the Cabinet and Frank's own experiences there had shown him how often an ability to bang a few heads together paid dividends. Graham Oyston was a little better, but only a little. If he hadn't got his fingers, and his reputation, burned early in his tenure at the Foreign Office with that shambles over Argentina, he would probably have been even worse than Hilary.

Frank didn't know what they wanted to talk about this morning, but he did not need to be an Einstein to have a pretty good idea. It would almost certainly be a discussion of possible options for dealing with the influx of Immigrants. The two Ministers would probably have thought out some plans for moving forward, but would want his OK before they started any visible action. That way, if there was an uproar in the house, they had made sure they at least had their backs covered. Frank had said himself when he was looking at No10 from the outside as he made his way up the political ladder that 'the buck stops there'. Now that he was 'there', it didn't seem such a clever phrase.

The third member of the meeting, the Minister for Education and Science, Eric Mercer, while not exactly a 'Dove' was sufficiently junior in post to still feel the need to defer to his senior colleagues – especially when they got up a head of steam – as was likely today. The other two would be quite prepared to steamroller him if he had any different views. The fact that they had wanted him in attendance probably meant that he had already been nobbled. Frank knew that if they went too far, he would have to stamp his own authority on the meeting without help from elsewhere.

* * * *

Colin's McLeod's views on religion closely mirrored his brother's, although he was a more gentle character. He saw room for repentance and forgiveness in areas where his elder brother saw only another sinner needing to be warned of impending judgment in the Heavenly Court. That difference of approach had led to arguments before in the McLeod household. Donald's move into the Manse next to Martin's Church had meant that those arguments were less frequent, but not any less severe when they happened.

There were no arguments of any substance between them, however, when they had come to discuss the proposal a few years ago from Church Headquarters, known by everyone in the movement as '121 George Street', the address in Edinburgh where the HQ was located, that the Church should allow practising Homosexuals to become Ministers. Colin had, by then, readily settled into both his work at the Nicolson Institute in Stornoway (known to the locals simply as the Nicolson) and his role as an Elder of the Church at Martin's itself. That position at School had given him perhaps a better platform to make judgments about homosexuality than his brother had. Seeing how 'his' youngsters had reacted to some of the stories which they had seen on their TVs at home, had shown him that there was a real need to protect people who had little in the way of worldly wisdom to help them in consideration of such issues. He felt strongly that it was up to the Church to take a stand that would show them that Homosexuality was something that was unnatural at the most basic physiological level. If such a way of living was to become prevalent, or (God help us!) a normal way to live our lives, then what hope did the human race have for the future?

Donald did not need convincing when he thought of the damage a practicing Homosexual could do as a Minister to his congregation! What were they thinking of? How could he maintain his fire and brimstone approach to living God fearing lives, while this was not only happening, but approved by the Church – *HIS* Church!

Wasn't it just typical, they both thought as they had returned to the Island after what had been one of the most difficult General Assemblies in recent times. The prevarication that had been apparent from, as Colin had put it, 'frightened men trying to avoid making frightening decisions' was inescapable. Donald was equally incensed. It was, he said, quite clear from the Bible what the approach of Christians should be on this. He quoted without needing to open the good book:

'Chapters 18 and 20 of Leviticus, which forms part of the Holiness code and lists prohibited forms of intercourse, contain the following verses:

Chapter 18 verse 22

"You shall not lie with a male as with a woman; it is an abomination."

Chapter 20 verse 13

"If a man lies with a male as with a woman, both of them have committed an abomination; they shall surely be put to death; their blood is upon them."

'Now' he raged, 'we're expected not only to accept this – this abomination, but also to allow our Ministers to preach its value from the pulpit. 'Cha bhith fhada's a tha mise nam mhinisteir, Colin,' he thundered 'anns an shaoghal agamsa'! ('Not while I'm Minister, Colin' – 'not in my world'!).

Their anger continued throughout that momentous journey home and, indeed lasted well into the night. It was something of a surprise to them both to find that, as they got into the part of the discussion 'what can we do about it', there was a considerable amount of agreement on that point too. As Colin left the Manse much later that night, he turned to Donald and said 'at least it has been good to be on the same side for a change, eh?'

* * * *

News travels fast and there are rarely any secrets which last for long on a small Island community, as is nearly always the case when everyone knows everybody else, or at least think they do. The next Kirk Session meeting after the brothers had returned from their trip to Edinburgh and the General Assembly meeting had been lively to say the least. Most of the Elders were already well aware of the main topic that was to be discussed. Voices normally so quiet, even when discussing quite emotional and emotive subjects, were raised in anger and disbelief.

Donald had found himself having to calm people down, so that others might have their say. That had been a first for him. It was if anything usually Colin who, in his role as Session Clerk, had to try and help Donald to remain calm in the face of views he would have liked to ride over.

'Donald' Colin had said on more than one occasion, 'there are times when you have to take the congregation with you, not just tell them how you are going to do things. If you can get them on your side, they are far more likely to respond positively. That, in turn, gives you an easier time afterwards if they truly feel that their point of view has been properly aired. You might even find once or twice that they come up with better ideas than you had.'

Donald had refused to believe that could be the case, but he had to admit he had not been ready for the ferociousness of the reaction amongst many of the Elders. Despite some of the differences in their views and what they had ended up discussing, they were of one accord when eventually, as Colin had known was inevitable, they came around to deciding what could be done about it. Almost the only light at the end of that tunnel was that the General Assembly had agreed that decisions of this nature should be left to individual Kirk

'Courts'. There, if it was felt that the 'revisionist' view that homosexuals were to be admitted to the clergy was the route they wanted to follow, they should be allowed to do so. Colin, and several of the Elders, felt that this was merely fudging the issue, when what was needed was clear leadership. He, and most of the others, felt that a stand needed to be taken, and if it was not taken now, it would never be taken.

It was, therefore, with a heavy heart that they agreed, almost unanimously, that their faith was no longer in safekeeping within the Church of Scotland. There were remarkably few objections when a vote was taken on a proposal, put forward by one of the more senior elders, to see if the group assembled in the room would be welcomed within the Free Church situated only a few yards away from their own building in the centre of the town. The Church, Donald had said in his closing remarks, would no doubt continue, but it would have to do so without the majority of the people in that room. It was clear that their beloved church was moving slowly, but inexorably, in a direction that none of the members, even those who might choose to remain in the present congregation, and buildings, were happy with. He, and those others who had now determined that they were to leave what had been their spiritual home, would be sad, but their faith would be the stronger because of what he described as a 'baptism of fire'.

5.

THE MAN STANDING in the searing mid-day heat of the Cairo Cemetery felt his life had now come to an abrupt end. His feelings, as he watched the caskets containing his family being lowered into the roughly hewn graves, were simply too great for him to think, or act rationally. He was so drained of emotion at the loss of his wife, his parents and his little boy, that he could not bring himself to rave and shout the way his people always did, in an effort to lessen their own grief. He wondered why this had happened. One senseless, emotionless, faceless act of terrorism meant that he had been robbed of his future and his family had been robbed of their lives.

He was known to his family, colleagues in the Cairo police force, and his friends as Deniz Mehmet. The African Brotherhood suicide bomber who had attacked the Mosque where his family had all been praying had died too, of course, but that did not lessen the pain he had felt by one iota. He wondered again at the turn of fate which had meant he had not been praying beside them inside the Mosque, even although he now knew that being there would have meant his own death.

The visit of a politician to the Police Station in Cairo where he was Chief Firearms Instructor, had seemed a good enough excuse at the time. He had never been a devoted practising Muslim as were the rest of his family, having seen too many deaths where anguished relatives had asked him the question 'how could Allah let this happen?' The usual Mullah's response of 'Allah is merciful, and we are not to question his actions, but accept that he has a greater purpose for them than we can fully understand' became an ever increasingly hollow incantation. The fact that most of these all too common atrocities were carried out by others who proclaimed themselves to be 'true believers' just made him all the more cynical in his own beliefs. He still knew he should have been with his family, and he also knew it was a burden he would carry to his own grave.

As he walked away from the cemetery on that dreadful afternoon, he felt there was no purpose to his life anymore. His wife would bear him no more children, and his son would never give him grandchildren to play with and bounce on his knee in his later years. As he stood at the side of the busy road in the centre of the city, he was ready to end it all. He had shed tears alone last night, rather than being able to sleep, and now felt completely drained. As the ancient bus rattled its way around the corner, he made to step out in front of it. Any pain would, he knew, be short lived, and then he could rejoin his beloved Dalmi, and his son Yousuf.

As his right leg started to move outwards, he felt the strong arm around his waist. A voice which whispered in his ear at the same time said 'I think there has been enough work for the gravediggers today, don't you?'

By the time he had looked around to see the face of the man who was holding onto him, the bus had gone past, and with it the moment. He was still in something of a trance, knowing just how near he had been to ending his own life, as he allowed the man to guide him to a seat at the nearby roadside café. He was alert enough, however, to realise that he had been steered towards a seat which did not give easy access back to the road he had so recently been going to step into.

When the man said 'coffee?' He could only nod dumbly. They sat in silence. Deniz could not bring himself to raise his eyes and look into the face of the man who had stopped him from ending his life underneath the wheels of a city bus. A few minutes later, as the waiter departed, having taken the order from the man sitting opposite him, he turned towards Deniz and said 'now tell me, what did you expect to achieve by ending your life like that, eh? If you had succeeded, Dalmi and your parents would never have been avenged, would they? Your hopes for Yousuf's future might have died with him, but he would have vanished from everyone's memories if you had taken your own life like that. Who else would remember the joy he had already given you and Dalmi? As long as there is someone on this accursed planet who remembers your name, you are not truly dead. Who else would remember Yousuf? Were you truly prepared to see all knowledge of his very existence eradicated from human memory? Did you care for him so little?'

The words shook Deniz. Not just because of the actual words that had been said but because, as they brought him slowly back from his state of shock, they also brought with them the realisation that this man, whoever he was, knew a great deal about him and his family. He had never seen him before, of that he was certain, but somehow the man knew about him. As his mind started to make the long slow climb back from the depths it had plumbed only a few minutes ago, he was already beginning to wonder how and why.

The man had waited until the coffee came before he said another word. As the waiter left their table, having delivered the hot bitter cups of liquid, he spoke again, this time without the vehemence he had earlier displayed.

'You are wondering who I am, and how I know about you?'

Deniz nodded and said nothing.

'My name is Omar Khalil, and I work in the recruitment centre of our beloved Cairo police force.' The word 'beloved' came out as something of a sneer. 'We have been keeping an eye on you for some time.'

Deniz still said nothing, but he looked up as he drank the first mouthful of the bittersweet coffee. Then he said slowly as his brain began to put meaning into what he was hearing. 'Who are '*we*'?

Omar smiled icily at Deniz. 'All in good time, my friend. The names of the people are not important. What is important is that we all share the same beliefs. I hope that in time you will feel able to call me friend, but there are some things which must come first.'

'There are an increasing number of people both here

in Egypt and elsewhere who are concerned at the way our religion is being used as an excuse for those whose aims are more territorial and secular. Their use of violence to achieve any of their aims was always regrettable, telling as it does the many non-believers in the world that Islam is a more violent way than the Quran itself allows. That mistaken view is now something that I and some others are not prepared to see continue unchecked.'

Deniz sipped his hot coffee slowly as he thought about that.

'What makes you think that I feel the same way as this?' Omar looked thoughtful for a moment, then said

'Just the odd word here and there have been reported to me as giving an indication that you have reservations about some of the things that have happened to our people, just as we do. You speak often as a father should rather than an adherent of any particular group. There are many in our land today who are easily led by others and as a result commit atrocities which are hateful in the eyes of Mohammed, as well as the Christian God. Most others are fearful of being overheard speaking against groups such as these because of the possibility of retribution. Someone who, as you have done, merely refuses to acquiesce quietly with some of these outpourings, stands out no matter how quietly they speak.'

Deniz understood what was being said. He also knew that he had been careful about when and where he had said anything about what was happening in the wider world. Dalmi had said on many occasions that he should be careful when he spoke about his true feelings – careful about when he was speaking and who he was speaking to. As a result he recognised that the only place where he had given any indication about how he felt was in the police station itself. There, over a coffee in the canteen, he had sometimes spoken to those he felt were of like mind. Even then he had been circumspect about what he actually said, always aware that there was the possibility that there might be informers among the groups of men who were supposed to be his colleagues. In the Egypt of today, the old adage 'a closed mouth catches no flies' was a good rule to follow.

He had been wary in those canteen chats of others who might report further up the line that he had different views to those elsewhere in the Police Force about some of the terrorist splinter groups who now operated with seeming impunity in many parts of his home city of Cairo, as well as elsewhere. Most of these groups were characterised by a preparedness to be as violent as necessary towards anyone who did not share their beliefs. It had never occurred to him that there were also those who felt the same as he did, and that they might also be on the lookout for those who shared their views.

Just like his father before him, he had originally joined the local Police Force because he recognised that there were many in the city of his birth who needed someone to look out for them. The old, the weak, the poor all needed to have someone to stand up for them and help them in their need. He had felt that he had a worthwhile rôle to play in keeping those poor unfortunates safe from the violence which surrounded them. Now he recognised with some shame that he hadn't even been able to protect his own family.

As he had listened to Omar giving a brief explanation of some of the things that he and his friends had already done, it cleared up several of the questions about mysterious recent deaths in the area. Deniz felt, as he listened, that the organisation fronted by the man sitting a few feet away from him might give him a perfect chance to exact some kind of revenge for the losses he had suffered that day. It was as if a light had started to shine through the gloom of his despondency. He felt good about that, even though he knew that some of those he might meet in the future, had played no part in the act which had taken his family from him.

It felt good to know that he might be part of an effort to rid the Earth of scum who would not hesitate to make war on women and children. If he could hasten some of them on their way to a final premature conversation with Allah, that too was good. They were part of a cancer which was turning his childhood playgrounds into areas where children were no longer safe and cared for. He didn't like that and, he realised, he needed to do something about it if he was ever going to be able to sleep soundly again at night.

6.

AS THE M.V. MARIANAS left the deserted stretch of coastline south of the Tunisian village of La Louza and slowly turned north, Adisa Folami briefly reflected on the sequence of events in his life which had led to him standing on the bridge and looking out to the Mediterranean. He knew about boats of course. His father had owned one when they lived in the small village of Kébir on the shores of the Red Sea. He had gone out with his father many times trying to catch enough fish, not only to feed the small family that was his two sisters and himself, but also make enough to do more than subsist.

It had been a hard, unrelenting struggle for them, just trying to survive in what was one of the poorest places on the planet. When his father announced that the family were leaving Eritrea and moving to Tunisia so that he could try and find work there, Adisa was not surprised. Somewhere else – almost anywhere else – must surely provide a better life for them all than this misbegotten and largely forgotten corner of the world. He had no option but to follow anyway. At thirteen years of age, he was too young, even in this country where it was the norm for children as young as six or seven to find ways of helping their families to survive, to do anything other than come along. As his father had said, there was nothing, absolutely nothing, they had to lose by making the move. It took several weeks walking, but that too was not unusual for people who counted a roof over their head as something of a luxury. Along the way they had come into contact with many others who lived along the North African shoreline. They had no more in the way of possessions than Adisa and his family, but he was struck by the fact that many did not hesitate to share what they had as he and his family passed through their villages. They would not have been able to make the trip if it had not been for the charity they had been shown, a charity that was an essential element of their Muslim faith.

* * * *

Adisa Folami knew that he would only be able to stay in this business for a limited time before he would have to move on. He had recognised that fact from the start of his involvement over ten years ago. The longer he continued to 'arrange' passage for others to head for the promised land that was the continent of Europe, the more likely it was that the net of European Police forces which were always working behind the scenes would find him. After the meeting a few weeks ago with the three men from Sudan he realised that such a move might be coming faster than he had expected. Abdul Rahman had sat down beside him as he was relaxing at his favourite coffee shop on the Rue Du Petit Souk, only a few yards away from the tourist centre – the Place de La Liberation – in the North Moroccan township of Larache, some 90 miles north of the bustling city of Rabat.

Until that meeting, he had been quite settled in his chosen work. He knew that the stream of people dubbed 'Economic Migrants' by western newspapers was likely to continue for the foreseeable future. That movement had started in the early years of the twenty-first century. At first it had been a trickle, then it became a flood of people trying to get away from the interminable warring in countries such as Yemen, Eritrea and Somalia. It quickly became something else as others from neighbouring countries such as Sudan and North African peoples from Chad, and even Kenya, showed themselves prepared to risk everything, including their lives, in an effort to find a better life for themselves and their families than they were suffering in their own country.

In those early days the sheer volume of people making the journey had almost swamped the Countries on the Northern shores of the Mediterranean. The much vaunted European Union had almost literally come apart at the seams as arguments raged among the member Countries on how to manage the vast numbers involved and, perhaps even more germane, who should pay for their continued presence.

Little by little however, they had found ways of coping. Now the southern coastlines of Italy, Greece and Spain were full of camps which had been set up as temporary shelters for the huge influx of men, women and children. Some of these 'temporary' camps had now been in existence for over twenty years, and were still full of a constantly changing population as more came to fill the spaces of others who had somehow managed to find a way of getting away from the camps and trying to lose themselves in the wider Continent.

That movement showed no signs of abating, even after all this time. As yet more European Countries tried to stem the flow of people from the African continent towards the rainbow they all saw gleaming in the north, the stepping off points had merely moved westward to find other avenues for exit. Once the land routes through Lebanon and on through Turkey had become too difficult, the migrants simply moved along the southern Mediterranean seaboard until they found an alternative route.

Libya, Tunisia and then Algeria had all seen their share of boats casting off into the darkness over recent years. When pressure was applied there, it was almost inevitable that Morocco would succumb in due course. That had taken a little longer to come about because sea transport had, at least in those early days, been so small that passage through the Straits of Gibraltar was a daunting task for everyone, even those who had nothing left to give or lose. Opening up Portugal and then the North Western Provinces of Spain as landing areas was not without risks. Even the most ignorant of people knew that the Atlantic is a more fearsome beast than the Mediterranean would ever be. This was, however, just another hurdle to be overcome by those who revelled in overcoming obstacles. Bigger boats – followed by bigger profits – inevitably followed.

Using larger vessels had meant that the carriers – he refused to see himself as a smuggler – had had to modify their approach a little. They could no longer move quite so close inshore before disgorging their human loads. Neither could the larger boats hang about. If the weather when they arrived at their drop off point was blowing a storm and running a high sea, it made no difference. Those making the trip knew the rules. The boat would send them off into the unknown, and then get the Hell away as fast as possible. He had explained to more than one group of terrified travellers that they did not want the authorities to have time to see exactly where they were launching their cargo of desperate humanity. If that happened, men with guns would be waiting in anticipation of their arrival at the shoreline and their trip to the Promised Land would terminate before it had even begun.

A whole variety of small inflatable craft were bought to provide that last link in the transportation chain, irrespective of their condition. Most were barely seaworthy, but then, it was only a one way trip wasn't it? These were quickly deployed to take them ashore, if they were lucky. He had seen more than one of these craft disappear beneath the waves within minutes of leaving the larger vessel. Most of the bodies would eventually reach their intended destination, but too late for their previous owners to use.

He had worked hard over the years building up a network of boat owners and others who were prepared to take risks and get through the various seaborne screens that Greece, then in turn, Italy and France, had erected to try and stem the flow. He had discovered that even the most daunting of problems for these owners was quickly resolved when money came into the discussion. As a result he had become known as someone who could make arrangements for such travel where others could not. He had grown rich on the pickings from that transport. Where some of the travellers got funds from to pay for an increasingly expensive passage for themselves and sometimes their whole families, he never knew and – he was honest enough to accept – cared even less.

Although he had never been involved himself, he knew that much the same had been happening in Northern Europe. Migrants who had started their journey in Africa, added to the many thousands who were coming westward from the further reaches of Eastern Europe had all ended up on that stretch of coastline where, on a good day, you could see the quaintly named White Cliffs of Dover from just a few miles away.

Why they were all so determined to reach Great Britain, he had never fully understood. Yes, he knew that the British people had always been ready to provide financial assistance from the day someone set foot ashore, while other countries made would-be settlers wait, sometimes for several years, before allowing such largesse. He also knew that, thanks to the days when the 'British Empire' had straddled the Globe like some latter day Colossus, there were huge numbers of people from Africa and elsewhere who already had relations over the channel. None of these fully accounted for the numbers he knew were trying, even after all this time, to make the journey.

It was just another thing he didn't fully understand, and as long as they kept coming – and paying – he didn't really care either. What he did care about however, was the request that Abdul Rahman had made so recently.

* * * *

7.

GEOFFREY WILLIAMS LOOKED out of the window of his private Gulfstream jet as it passed over the rump of Scotland that contained North Berwick en route to yet another touchdown at Lakenheath in Norfolk. He sighed again at the thought of the way his world had changed in the last six years. Since he had been awarded the Nobel Prize for Physics his world had changed beyond recognition. Whereas before he had been a 'laboratory animal' spending the vast majority of his time in his labs in the complex south of Cambridge, he now saw them no more than a few days in any month. The rest of the time he either spent explaining to Ministers and other officials some of the technical details behind his revolutionary work on positioning technology, or flying somewhere to explain to others the uses that he could see for this new branch of science.

Last month had had spent three days out of his busy schedule to explain to Authorities in Spain how domestic animals out on the hills could, when implanted with his new transmitters, be found without the need for extensive searches on foot. Animals such as these were often left to fend for themselves during the winter, and needed to be brought in for calving and general husbandry in the spring.

His technology made that job so much easier. Today, he was returning from a very similar exercise with the Laplanders. The animals were very different there, of course, but the technology didn't know that.

The second area of research which had proven to be so interesting had come about almost by accident. While examining the problems associated with finding animals out on the hills with his GPS improvements, one of his team had come up with a suggestion that they might be able to use the same technological links to 'persuade' the animal to come down voluntarily. That was still not solved to his satisfaction, but they were already making progress.

He knew he had just been in the right place at the right time to take advantage of the other advances which were being developed at the same time. If he had not decided to sit down beside that particular young scientist at that particular scientific conference at – now where had it been? – oh yes, that was it , The Haven Hotel on the edge of Poole harbour, none of this might have happened. At least, he was prepared to admit to himself, none of it would have happened to him. Certainly, he had been the one able to see before others where the technologies discussed at that lunchtime chat could be combined, and where they could bring about changes which might be useful in the wider society. Nevertheless, he had only played a small part in the technological advances themselves which had made it all possible. His speciality had been – still was, he tried to remind himself wryly – GPS technology.

To the man in the street, GPS still meant not much more than a Satellite Navigation screen sitting above the front console of his latest car. Front edge technology was, as usual, much more advanced than anything the ordinary man could buy at his local Halfords before embarking on a road trip to Europe for his annual family holiday. Specific Personal Positioning Systems (SPPS) were now available, thanks to his pioneering work in the field, which could allow someone at the other end of the transmitted signals to place an object as small as a Bumble Bee to within a few nanometres. Centimetres and even millimetres were now measures of the past when it came to talking distances.

His work on Miniaturisation was another element to the thesis which had led to his Nobel Prize. Transmitters, and indeed cameras, could now be produced which themselves were no larger than a pin head. Admittedly it was still a large pin head, but he knew that ongoing work on an even greater degree of miniaturisation would improve on even that limitation in the next few months.

He knew he had benefitted financially beyond either his needs or indeed his wildest hopes as a result of the breakthrough in technology which had allowed him to create what was now increasingly seen as the perfect tool for keeping track of criminals and their whereabouts, without the need for expensive incarcerations. He had initially disdained the material side of the venture that his wife had set up with him as a non-executive co-director to patent and then manufacture the hardware that was now coming into widespread use across Europe and elsewhere. He had entered the scientific community because of a love of science or, as one of his old tutors at Oxford had described it, 'a search for the truth'. Gradually, however, he had come to like the ease which the money had conferred on their way of life. The Gulfstream was just one of those. The large gated house on the outskirts of the sleepy Suffolk village of Worlington was another. He could now afford to go anywhere in the world for a holiday, but had still not managed that simple exercise in the last ten years.

When he had sat down beside that young scientist by the name of Neil Franklin, he had listened with some excitement to what the young man had to say. Neil, it turned out, was one of Stephen Hawkins' assistants in Cambridge, and was nearing his own breakthrough in a quite different technology. His speciality, hardly surprising when you took into account who his mentor had been, was in finding ways of non verbal communication between man and machine.

They had not, at that point, developed any sophisticated hardware to carry the project forward, but they were already able to think of an action as simple as changing the channels on a specially adapted Television set and have it happen. They used modified headphones to convey the transmission signals to the hardware, but were looking for ways to improve the system which would relieve them of the need for such a bulky method of communicating. The neural links had all been identified and were capable of providing the necessary instructions, not only to the specially adapted TVs but also to do such simple things as switching a kettle on – and off. Further, and more sophisticated methods were, according to Neil, merely a matter of simple mathematical extrapolations and then programming of the theoretical work already done.

In the way known to scientists the world over, they had got into such a deep discussion that the conference organiser had to come looking for them at the start of the afternoon session. They had however reached the point where it was obvious to Geoffrey that one of the severe limiting factors in the potential application of Neil's ideas was one of distance. It had never occurred to Neil's group that if they could send these messages over a long distance (much further than they were even trying to do at the moment) there might be a far greater use for the technology. Bluetooth technology was useful in much the same way, but carried with it much the same limitations.

Geoffrey with his SPPS hat on, could see that there might be a far greater use in society if the two ends of the communication link did not have to be in the same room. He had felt at the time that there was a great significance to what the young scientist was trying to achieve, but the conference organiser had called a premature halt to that discussion, and they had gone their own separate ways afterwards. He had since been too caught up in his own work to think other than fleetingly about the potential uses and benefits that had been raised in his mind during that chance meeting.

The changes that his development of SPPS technology had brought about had not been universally welcomed, with all manner of objections from vested interests. One of the earliest uses for SPPS had come from the Army. Soldiers at the front – Geoffrey reminded himself that there was always a 'front' somewhere in the world they now lived in – were able to wear wristbands which enabled them to be found quickly if they became separated from their unit in the heat of a squad battle. They could now be traced very quickly by rescuers if they were injured, sometimes even 'lost' as the firefight moved elsewhere. As is always the case, however, the other side just as quickly became aware of what the bands were capable of doing.

The loss of several members of a 'rescue' operation which had been set in motion after two soldiers had been captured following a gun battle, was something that Commanders in the field would not accept as a regular outcome from the new technology. Once it had become clear that an ambush had been set by the simple expedient of placing a captured armband hidden from sight but within view and range of the enemy's own troops (and guns), things had changed almost overnight. The part of his thesis dealing with miniaturisation had shown that technology now existed which allowed such a transmitter to be implanted into a subject using an ordinary injection. There was thus no real objection from anyone when soldiers were given one of these more recently developed implants to keep track of their whereabouts on the field of battle. After all, who would want to be captured by an enemy whose disregard for human life had been at the very core of the fight they were involved in?

He still remembered the heated discussions that had taken place with some of the Country's highest ranking officers then. They were quite cold blooded about some of the aspects of the new technology. When he had said that the implant could be given easily enough into the upper arm, they were literally up in arms at the suggestion! 'It just won't do!' one of the Lieutenant Commanders had said – Geoffrey seemed to remember he had been from the marines – 'it is quite possible that an arm could get damaged or even blown off in a firefight, then how could we find them?' Geoffrey had to admit that he hadn't thought of it quite like that.

In the end, they had decided that somewhere near the top of the spine was the optimum placement. It made no difference to the transmitter's effectiveness, and as another Army man had said 'if they get hit there, there is little point in expending precious resources trying to recover a dead body.'

The decision taken to exchange the old 'TAG' system of keeping track of the whereabouts of prisoners who were out on licence, for the newer and much more sophisticated electronic bug implanted as part of the condition of their release had, however, caused much more of an uproar.

Perhaps naturally enough, prisoner support groups had come out against what they described as a flagrant breach of an individual's human rights. Arguments that implants would only be inserted after agreement with the individual, and that they would be time limited to the length of the sentence imposed by the Courts, after which they would either be removed surgically, or allowed to wither and die in the case of the even newer organic based devices, cut no ice with the protesters. They were joined on the protest lines by a myriad of other interest groups, some with diametrically opposite views of the issues. Standing shoulder to shoulder with the 'Human Rights Campaigners' were those who felt that the use of micro-electronic implants were unacceptable, because they allowed the release of violent individuals, rapists and serial paedophiles, back into the community rather than being kept away from 'their children'.

The picket lines which sprang up outside the research buildings almost inevitably included students from across the social spectrum. Those students, had they but known it, turned out to be one of his best allies when Geoffrey got down to discussions in the corridors of power. There, the very fact that students were so obviously, and sometimes violently, against what was happening, became a cause of raised eyebrows and smiles of disdain. One of the more senior members of the Administration (in the Home Office of all places) even went as far as to say, 'if the students are so against this, then we must be doing something right – off the record of course!'

Other objectors had included the hierarchy within a number of other Government Departments. Mandarins and perhaps less surprisingly – the largely privatised Prison Service itself – saw years of empire building reduced to dust almost overnight. Many of them expressed reservations about the validity of the new technology.

They were not above using the same moral arguments as those standing in the rain outside, even though their motives might have been more prosaic. It was clear from the outset that the numbers of staff needed to oversee the new systems being put in place to monitor prisoner movement 'in the community' were only a fraction of what was needed to contain them in secure prisons. The sums of money which had been assessed as being capable of release through the new measures however, meant that no-one in Government, apart from the Prison Service itself, had any desire to oppose the changes for any length of time. Other Government Departments were already casting envious eyes over the figures and wondering how easy it would be to slide some of the savings into their own Departmental budgets. Geoffrey remembered with some pleasure sitting on the sidelines while some of those dog-fights broke out with increasing frequency and venom as the full level of the monies involved became clearer.

With those objections had started a campaign of personal vilification which persisted to this day. Wherever he went nowadays, he was followed by the press looking for what they always termed as 'human interest' for articles. It was in reality a sustained attempt at creating some kind of monster for their readers, of the man credited with introducing 'Robotic Supervision' – the popular name given by the press to his technology. In his mind it was nothing of the sort, of course, but he had long ago given up trying to reason with people who were manifestly unreasonable.

It was the continuing disruption that those of a similar persuasion were creating that was now forcing an ordinary businessman such as he saw himself, to use an Air Force base as his destination rather than somewhere like Heathrow as other members of the public did. At least he knew that the USAF would not allow swarms of protesters to get too close when greeting his arrival back in his home country. There was, these days, always a few protesters ready to hurl insults, and a few other things, at any car that sped through the gates, in either direction. They did so on the grounds that anything attached to the military had to be something they would not like. But they, he knew, would be kept at a safe distance.

The darkened windows meant that no-one would see who was inside, but the very fact that they were travelling through one of the American staffed, but British owned, airbases was enough to give some a reason to vent their spleen at whoever was in the sleek limousine as it turned right at the roundabout on Lord's Walk and disappeared into the green English countryside. The round trip (security again! he thought) took them back around the airbase and onto the A11 heading south, before heading to his home in Worlington.

8.

Sandra Wilson had always wanted to be a Primary Teacher, ever since her own schooldays in Dunvant, on the outskirts of Swansea. She had decided as far back as that, that helping children to read, write and become happy members of the adult community, was something she wanted to be part of. Now, as the newly appointed Head Teacher at the small Primary School set in the village of Cwmfelinfach a few miles north of Newport, she was beginning to have second thoughts.

It wasn't as if she had fallen out of love with teaching. Quite the opposite, in fact. As she had gained experience in her teaching career, she saw ever more clearly the need for a sensitive approach to helping children at an early age to reach their full potential. That wasn't easy, sometimes because of home environments that weren't helpful and sometimes because the individual child had learning difficulties. Sometimes it was both. The need for a highly individualistic approach was borne in on her every day if she and her staff were to be successful in bringing the best out of all the children – recognising that each child's 'best' might be very different. That, at the end of the day, was what they were supposed to be doing, wasn't it?

Her concerns were much more because she now saw a great deal more of the non-teaching side than she had before. She had already known about the regular meetings where she, along with other Head Teachers, would be given 'guidance' about the latest changes to the curriculum. That was understood as being a vital part of their job.

What she had not been so aware of, was the amount of pressure being put on teachers to apply standards to the classroom which were simply non-enforceable in some cases. No allowance was made for differing situations and circumstances that each school had to deal with on a daily basis. Just getting the kids into school on time was sometimes a real problem when the school was situated in a small rural position like hers where transport was a difficult issue for some of the parents. Then there were the interminable changes to, well, nearly everything, as one Government 'initiative' followed another. It seemed to her as if these were nearly always thought up by someone sitting behind a desk in Whitehall who had not seen the inside of a classroom since their own far off schooldays.

She smiled grimly to herself as she looked again at one of the sheets handed out at yesterday's meeting. The Councils couldn't even get the same title for those with ostensibly the same rôle in education. The sheet showed the hierarchies in the Local Authority Education Departments throughout Wales. None of the areas were organised the same! And this from an organisation that wanted all Schools to be shoe-horned into a 'one size fits all' approach! At least here in

Caerphilly the top post was called Chief Education Officer. Elsewhere it ranged from 'Director of People (a bit too near the truth to be funny, she thought) and Head of Lifelong Learning' all the way through to 'Corporate Director – Education & Transformation', whatever the Hell that meant!

There was nothing funny, however, about one of the other sheets handed out. It showed how all the primary schools in the district rated against the new 'colour coded' regime which apparently gave rankings against each school in what someone had considered the important elements of primary education. The latest view, she thought. And she would not be surprised to find that it would all be changed in the near future, if not at the next meeting. She didn't like feeling like that. It wasn't the way she wanted to feel about her job. But, she recognised, there was precious little she could do about it. One of the more senior teachers at a previous meeting had tried to object to the continual changes and the almost as frequent u-turns, and had been put down very quickly and very publicly.

This latest sheet said that Cwmfelinfach, along with most of the other village schools running up the Sirhowy Valley from Newport up to Blackwood, were being classified as 'red' which was apparently the lowest ranking available in the new system. They had been told that they must improve. Full stop. When one or two of the others had tried to find out how the figures had been compiled, they were unsuccessful. The man from the Education & Lifelong Learning Directorate in Ystrad Mynach had said they were being prepared in the same way across the whole of England and Wales, and there was absolutely no point in trying to make some kind of alteration to the methods used just for our area, especially when the obvious reaction would be that we were merely trying to find a way of putting a better gloss on what was a very bad assessment.

He had gone on to say that it was felt that a great deal of the problems arose because of the general low level of behaviour that many children in these areas demonstrated. When he was asked to explain how he drew that conclusion, he said that information had been drawn from a host of other services across the region, youth clubs, children's services, social work service etc. These all showed that there was a large proportion of what he called dysfunctional families in the area. Many of those families had primary age children as part of the family unit. Difficulties highlighted elsewhere said clearly that there was a problem with behaviour which needed to be addressed. Schools, particularly Primary Schools, needed to be able to demonstrate that they were playing a full part in dealing with this kind of problem.

Like most of the others at the meeting, Sandra was not convinced by the arguments put forward. Yes, of course, there were sometimes problems. They were after all children and not adults they were dealing with. There were also, it was recognised by all the teachers at the meeting, some problem families. These were however well known by each teacher, and in no case, were they in anything like a majority. There was quite a discussion about that item on the agenda. She had said that she felt it was a little like giving a dog a bad name, and doing so without any real evidence. A number of her colleagues agreed with that, but it made no difference to the man at the head of the table.

Now that she was back behind her own desk, she knew she would have to be seen to do something about the information shown in the charts. She just didn't know what that might be.

9.

GARETH THOMAS SIGHED as he switched off the engine of his van and got out at the end of what had been another long day fixing other people's car problems. As he went inside the small house he shared with his childhood sweetheart Madeleine – Maddie he had always called her – and their three children at number 24 Pratt Street in the even smaller South Wales village of Cwmfelinfach, he thought that all his days recently seemed to be long and tiring. He went through into the kitchen and started to clean the dirt accumulated over the day out of his fingernails.

Car mechanics were no longer as plentiful in this part of the South Wales valleys as they had been when his father and grandfather had set up their original businesses over fifty years ago. Increasing dependence on computerised systems in nearly all cars nowadays instead of the previous 'hands on' work had reduced his clientele to those who could not afford the newer more modern vehicles which most families either now had, or wanted. They still had the body repair premises on the edge of the light Industrial Estate outside Cwmcarn. Even there, however, business was starting to fall off.

There was, thankfully, a substantial number of the older generation who still had a distrust of anything that was done solely by machines. This latter group made up more than seventy percent of Gareth's customers. They all wanted to have someone to chat to while work on their increasingly decrepit cars was being carried out. As a result, he spent more time with them than was strictly necessary, but he regarded it as a worthwhile investment for his business. He knew that it meant that they would more than likely be on the phone – his phone – again when their next emergency came along.

They were now one of the oldest firms in the area, with a reputation for customer care which had always served them well in the past and, he hoped, would continue to serve them well into the future. The business had been originally established by his paternal grandfather 'Bampie'. His father had gone on to develop it beyond both the older man's dreams and capabilities. Bryn Thomas had always had an eye for the main chance, and he had been the one to push the body shop venture. He had felt it would draw in more business than just the mechanical repair unit would ever do. When a smaller garage went under in the village of Risca a few miles down the Sirhowy Valley, but crucially much closer to the Newport conurbation, he saw an opportunity to expand the business even further, and at much less cost to himself than would otherwise have been the case. He had been on the point of opening up that second set of premises when things came apart. The world wide recession in the early part of the century had destroyed his father's hopes of becoming both a major player in the South Wales Garage fraternity and any hopes he had had of becoming really wealthy.

The firm still served a fairly large part of what had always been described as 'The Valleys'. The logo 'Valley Mobile Mechanics' picked out in gold lettering along each side of his van decorated with the red Welsh Dragon symbol, was testament to that service. The business had, however, never reached the scale his father had initially hoped and dreamed of.

Bryn, his father, was a difficult man to live with at the best of times. Gareth remembered with some anger the way he had always ridden rough-shod over everyone when things didn't go his way, and that didn't just apply to those who worked for him. Whenever something didn't go according to plan – his plan – then someone else was going to be blamed, and it was never Bryn himself who was at fault. He was always more concerned with finding someone to blame than in trying to resolve whatever the problem might be. Gareth and his younger brother Peter had quickly reached an understanding that when their father was in one of those – all too frequent – moods, they stayed away from him as much as they could. Most of the other members of the family stayed away from him too, but Gareth and Peter could not close the front door and walk away as the other members of the family could – and did.

There had been even less escape for his mother. She had stood the incessant rows and humiliations that the marriage had become as long as she could, but once she felt the boys were nearly grown up, she had left in tears as well. The final straw had come with the unexpected late pregnancy which happened when Gareth and his brother were already in their early teens. Gareth remembered only too vividly the accusations and recriminations which had flown between his parents during the months that the fifth member of the family was on the way. He could never be certain, of course, but he had no doubts that the atmosphere that had been present throughout that unfortunate time had been closely linked with the final outcome.

When the baby was still-born and had arrived two months prematurely, his father was incandescent. The fact that the baby would have been a little sister for the two boys, rather than another brother seemed to make matters worse. On one never to be forgotten occasion, his father had actually said 'so you've killed my daughter!' as he shouted in the middle of another of the seemingly interminable arguments which had been the family norm at that time. Gareth, young as he was, knew then that the writing was on the wall for the family as a unit.

His mother had retreated to the spare room after that particular shouting match and eventually left to stay temporarily with a friend who lived not far away. When she had eventually left the area to find a new life for herself in Hampshire, the boys had both been distraught. They were, however, old enough to realise that she saw no future for herself while anywhere close to the old man. He had tried to control what she did even after she had moved out, through his contacts in the area. When she found out that he was keeping tabs on almost her every movement, she knew she had to put a real distance between herself and the rest of the family, no matter how difficult that might be.

Gareth knew she had wanted to take both of her boys away at the same time as she was leaving, but his father had 'struck a deal' with her which ensured she could continue to have a reasonable standard of living, beyond the minimum the legal system would have given her, provided he kept the boys. Peter – always the apple of his mother's eye – couldn't wait to get closer to his mother, however, and further away from the man who didn't have any awareness of the effects he had on those around him. When Peter was contemplating moving onto University after school, he had made sure he went to one in the South of England. That was partly because he would then be close to where their mother now lived in Hampshire and also partly so that he could only rarely get 'home' at weekends while also studying. As a consequence, he didn't have to explain why he didn't keep in touch as much as the old man demanded.

It wasn't surprising in the circumstances, that continuing contact between the two brothers was haphazard, to say the least. Geography has always been a great killer of relationships and their family unit was not immune from that problem. Peter had had his studies and Gareth was making the business as profitable as possible. Gareth was both surprised, and a little disappointed to hear from the occasional phone calls they managed to make to each other, that Peter was losing his South Wales accent very quickly. He remarked on the changes on one occasion, and Peter laughed and said 'it's the best way, really. Even one or two of the tutors have said they have difficulty sometimes in knowing what I'm saying, and a couple of the other students made it very plain that they somehow see it as a 'lower class accent' as if it says that I'm not quite as clever as they are.'

Gareth, for some reason that he had difficulty putting into words, felt hurt – not so much by the attitudes spoken about – but by Peter's reaction to them. By the time Peter had completed his University Studies at Southampton, gaining a 1st Class Honours in Molecular Biology, and moved on to a Government Research post based in Godalming just south of Guildford in Surrey, you would not have known that he had come from anywhere other than the South of England.

Their father was always telling them, and anyone else who still cared to listen, how much he loved his family. There were occasions, Gareth thought, when the old man perhaps even believed it. As he had proved on many an occasion, however, his words and his actions only came together occasionally, and then only when there was an ulterior motive somewhere. His normal response when asked to help someone he knew was 'what's in it for me?' Perhaps, Gareth often thought, he just didn't care enough about anybody except himself. Whatever the motivation, the result was much the same. It had been left to Gareth to stay and keep the old man happy, or try to.

Bryn was still nominally in charge of the business, although he had 'wound down' his involvement in recent years. He had moved into local politics after his wife had gone – more as a way of filling the void in his life that he had discovered, than any real political conviction. He now spent more time at the Town Hall in Newport than he did at the garage. He had even managed to get himself elected onto the Council Education Committee which all helped to give him an alternative interest to his waning involvement in the family business. All the major business decisions – and most of the hard work, Gareth thought to himself – were now made by Gareth, and had been for some time. That made for a reasonably comfortable living for him and his family, as long as he put the hours in.

His father, now about to turn sixty, had not mellowed with the years, however, and Gareth recognised that it was far too late to expect the old man to change. Like all the others, he and his family kept the old man at arms length as much as possible. Maddie in particular was always threatening 'to give him a piece of my mind' whenever they visited him. Gareth just wanted an easy life, however, and he hoped he could continue to keep a lid on what was an ever present sore in their lives.

He had just got his hands wet when a squeal made him turn around. 'Daddy, Daddy' his daughter Samantha shouted as she ran into the kitchen and hugged him. 'Hello sweetheart' he laughed as he lifted her and returned the hug. He and Maddie, his wife, had thought that their family was complete when the two boys Nathan and then Daniel had been born ten and eight years ago. She had even gone back to work on a limited hours basis at her old Primary School in Ynysddu in the next village. It had been more than a shock when they discovered that another child was on the way. Samantha had proven to be an absolute gem of a daughter, and they both had high hopes for her – if she was allowed to develop in her own way – he thought wryly.

It was his usual routine, when he got home early enough, to play with Sam for a little while and then give her a bath, before she went to bed. Maddie and he had agreed that this was a good way to let the little girl know that he loved her, even if he could not spend as much time with her as her mother did.

10.

DENIZ MEHMET'S ABILITIES with firearms meant that when he started to be involved with Omar's group, he was quickly seen as a valuable member of the effort. It didn't take long after he had agreed to join Omar's cadre of people to be asked to carry out one or two smaller operations for the group who operated behind the scenes of Cairo's Police Force.

On one occasion he had been tasked with (as Omar had phrased it) 'disinfecting' a coffee shop where a group of the self-same African Brotherhood was known to spend time. The other member of Omar's group who had been assigned to that action had said afterwards that he had rarely seen anyone enjoy using the AK47 as much as Deniz had. Those kinds of stories became ever more lurid as they were repeated, and soon the word within the group was that you did not mess with him, even if his name was not known to many.

He lived for the next operation. It had taken some time, but as he had become more and more useful to the shadowy organisation which Omar had introduced him to, opportunities to take out a few more members of the African Brotherhood had presented themselves. He remembered with particular satisfaction the bomb making factory that had been uncovered on the outskirts of the city near to the airport. As he had walked in unannounced through the front door of the building he had time to see the expressions on the faces of those inside. He fondly imagined that the surprise he had seen there was no more than his own family had suffered in the supposed comfort of their Mosque. He had no problems either with the realisation, as he pulled the trigger, that two of the bomb makers were women – after all his wife and his mother had not been spared when they had been a target, were they?

Of course, success at one 'elimination' had led to others. At his now regular meetings with Omar (he had checked after that first fateful meeting, and he did actually work in the recruitment section of the HQ, and his name WAS Omar) he had never been able to find out more about anyone else who was also doing the same work as he was. He had asked once or twice, but Omar had said that the fewer names he knew, the safer it would be for everyone – including Deniz himself. The less he knew of names and faces, the less he could tell if he were ever to fall into the 'wrong' hands. Deniz understood that, and so hadn't pressed the issue.

As time went on, however, occasions arose where he had to work with others on particular assignments, and so he came to know that, even within the confines of the Cairo police force there was a significant number of people whom Omar used from time to time. Conversations about anything other than the operation they were involved in was however almost non-existent, and so now – even some time later –

Deniz barely knew the names of no more than a handful of others.

Then, at one of the their meetings in that same coffee shop where it had all begun, Omar had asked him if he would like to be part of a major operation which they had decided needed to be put in place. As he heard some of the details, he recognised that here was a once in a lifetime opportunity to wreak havoc amongst those who had caused him so much grief. He had resigned his position within the police force almost immediately, and moved to a different part of the City. There, Omar had said, was the area controlled by the African Brotherhood. He would be charged with getting 'inside' the organisation – and then waiting. When he asked what he was waiting for, Omar merely said 'to be available for action as and when they determined was the best time to 'take out' some of the leaders. It is always relatively easy to remove the foot soldiers. If we are to have a very real effect on the group, we need to aim higher.'

He now lived in a shadowy world where cryptic messages in coffee shops and whispered conversations on street corners were enough to give him a renewed purpose in life.

This latest assignment would probably be his last. He knew that. Going 'underground' over the last three years had not been easy, but as Omar had said 'there are some people who are so well protected that a stranger cannot just walk into a bar and 'eliminate' them. They are continually surrounded by others whose sole purpose in life is to prevent exactly such an event. There is only one way to deal with those in such a position – become so near to them and so indispensible – that being nearby is something that they not only expect, but welcome. That takes time.'

Deniz had no problems with that. He had no family to leave behind, no friends who would notice and perhaps remark on the fact that he had dropped out of their lives. Deniz had never heard of Ahmed Chisisi before, but when Omar remarked that he had it on good authority that he had been the one who had planned that long ago atrocity at the Mosque, it merely, to Deniz' mind, sealed the man's fate. All that remained was to go into the details of how and when. He felt even better when Omar had said that there would be no further face to face contact between them. Any future contact between them would be when, and only when, Deniz himself felt he was ready. Then, and only then, would Omar determine the next course of action. Until then, Deniz would be entirely in control of his future actions. For the foreseeable future Deniz Mehmet would cease to exist. Yousuf Kanté would take his place – a constant reminder to him of the little boy who had been so cruelly taken from him.

* * * *

Sandra Wilson was beginning to wonder if the decision she had made all those years ago to help Primary school children grow into responsible adults had been a mistake. Coming out of the latest meeting with officials of the

County Education Department, she was seething. The newly appointed chairman of the Council Committee with oversight of Schools (a Mr Bryn Thomas) had made it crystal clear that the present scenario of misbehaviour amongst the Primary age group across the County needed to be tackled.

When she, and others, had asked how they were supposed to do that, he replied 'find a way. If you can't, then I will find a way for you, whether you like it or not. I have been told that our budget for next year will be heavily influenced by what we do in this area. Low performance will lead to less money, just like in any other business. You have no more than three months from now for the statistics we collect to show a marked improvement. If not then you can stand aside while I take whatever action I consider necessary.'

James, Sandra's husband, was English. He had obtained his degree in Medicine from Swansea University and met the strawberry haired blonde at one of the parties there. It had been love at first sight and they had never regretted tying the knot as soon as their separate degree courses were finished. While he had slotted into the General Practice on the outskirts of Newport, he was not blind to the different way the Welsh people viewed the world. He was proud of his own English background and, apart from anything else, he felt it often gave him a wider perspective on events than those who had never lived anywhere else except in the Principality.

When she had come in foaming at the mouth at Bryn Thomas's comments, he had only been able to quieten her down after she had drunk two Vodka Cokes. For someone who only very rarely imbibed, that was a clear demonstration of how uptight she was. Sitting her down, he said 'tell me'.

As he listened, he could understand her concerns, but he said 'what, in practical terms can he do?' She didn't have an answer to that.

'Then don't you think you are jumping at shadows a little darling?'

'Maybe', she said, 'but why was he so dogmatic? He must see, surely, that there has to be a great many reasons for the problem. It's not as if all the schools have the same level of indiscipline. Depending on the catchment area for the intakes, some schools have a bigger problem than others. Then there is the actual number of teachers that each school has and their individual levels of experience. Some schools in the 'better' areas can get teachers with no problem, but others have to make do with whoever is prepared to go and work there. Then teacher turnover comes into it as well. If you are continually losing teachers – for all kinds of reasons, pregnancy, long term sickness and teachers moving away because of husbands job moves – then one school may well have a significantly different set of problems to the one down the valley.'

'You're getting yourself all worked up again, sweetheart.'

'You're damned right I am. This approach of 'one size fits all', is simply and utterly wrong. What can I, what can any of us, do about it to try and change his mind?'

11.

GORDON MORRISON LAY back in bed and snuggled up to Rachel. He sometimes wondered when he awoke early like this, how he had ever come to live in a small Welsh seaside town like Barmouth. Hailing from the West Coast of Scotland as he did, it constantly amazed him how different parts of the world could be so similar, once you scratched under the surface.

It all seemed so far away now: his beginnings on the Island of Benbecula situated between South and North Uist in the Outer Hebrides. The island is also known in Gaelic poetry as *An t-Eilean Dorcha* "the dark island", and during the long winter months, that name seemed to be a particularly apt one. His parents had, at that time, run a small Bed & Breakfast business south of Culla Bay, one of the most picturesque stretches of sand in the whole island. Guests were few and far between. When they existed, they were nearly always birdwatchers or walkers, neither of whom were renowned for spending money. His mother had managed to supplement their income and make enough to remain on the Island by working a few hours a week at the nearby airport.

The island was, for the most part, a flat piece of ground with many deep indenting sea water lochs as well as those of the landlocked freshwater variety. Very few people, fewer roads and even fewer jobs. Whenever he was out with his mum and dad in the car, his father would say as they passed another vehicle, 'this is what passes for the rush hour here'. He remembered being asked to help cook breakfast for the guests from a very early age. By the time he was nine or so, he was also taking charge of the kitchen for the main meals, whenever his mother had to make another visit to the doctor. She had made those at regular intervals, but it wasn't until she needed hospital treatment that he realised just how sick she was. She died from the cancer that was plaguing her some six weeks after he celebrated his tenth birthday.

If he had been the only child, his father had said at the time, they would have stayed and tried to make the business work. Two children, one of whom was a little girl, just seven years old, made that hope an impossibility. They did struggle along for some months – what else was there to do? – until his father managed to sell the remote house they lived in and announced that they were moving to Stornoway on the Isle of Lewis. There he had managed to buy a slightly larger B&B at a reasonable price, mainly because the owners hadn't managed to make ends meet themselves. As his father had said at the time, what else did he know that could support a family? At least they had neighbours there who could, and did, help with the raising of the two children, especially his little sister Pat.

The move, taking place when it did, helped him in his studies. He had already begun the discussions with his father about what might be his options for a secondary school education that could avoid him leaving the island. The latest family developments took that decision out of their hands. The decision instead became one of which subjects he might take at the Nicolson in Stornoway itself. With the help of one of the tutors there, he and his father had eventually decided that the young Gordon Morrison would take Business Management and Accounting with the addition of Home Economics. He had already decided in his own mind that he liked the idea of running his own B&B or perhaps even a small Hotel.

His first few lessons in Home economics were not easy! He remembered with some dismay the jibes the rest of the class (all girls he discovered!) put his way. It wasn't until after the settling in dance/disco, that things improved. This was run by the Institute to help pupils who might have been very isolated in their home environments to gel with others from the patchwork of islands. Many of them were only now realising that others existed who had very different views on just about everything they cared to discuss.

He had found himself at that early get-together standing beside the trestle table that passed for a bar (soft drinks only of course), at the same time as a girl who smiled at his obvious discomfort, when he was asked by the woman behind the makeshift shelf, to specify what flavour of lemonade he would like. When he said 'blackcurrant please', she smiled and said 'that's my favourite too' and extended her hand to introduce herself as Rhona McLeod. It was the start of a brilliant friendship.

Rhona was one of those people who were the life and soul of any party they attended. He had never met anyone quite like her. She and her extended family were well known in Stornoway. One of her uncles was a Minister in the town and another taught Gaelic at the Nicolson Institute itself. She quickly took Gordon under her wing and, as a result, all the jibes and any other difficulties for the youngster who knew nobody else in the school, disappeared. It would not be any form of exaggeration to say that those initial few minutes with a blackcurrant flavoured lemonade changed his whole experience of school.

Over the next few years the two of them became inseparable. Their studies never merged, of course. Rhona was doing Chemistry and Biology and, Gordon knew, doing extremely well. He had overheard two of the teachers talking about her when he had gone into the staff room unannounced on one occasion. They felt she showed 'great promise' and 'could go right to the top' if she 'put her mind to it'. He didn't tell her that. He felt it might make her even more certain than she already seemed, that her future lay beyond the Island.

He knew most people would have called it 'puppy love' and, looking back on it now as he snuggled into Rachel's warmth, he was honest enough to know that was a fairly correct description. At the time it hadn't felt like that, though. He had promised her when the parting did eventually come, that he would always be available for her if she ever needed help. She need have no fear of that. He felt an enormous sense of gratitude for the way she had been there for him when he needed it most. The least he could do was return the favour.

He had no illusions about his own academic abilities. When he started at The Nicolson, he already had the idea that he would become some kind of landlord. His ambitions had never been loftier than that. His father had been more than happy to have him 'on the staff' at his own B&B. His father had made something of a success of it, and it didn't take him long to start saying things about needing another pair of hands. By that time, however, Gordon was beginning to have other ideas. They might not have been great things, but they were his things, not his father's. Life on the island was pleasant, but some of Rhona's views had rubbed off on him. He wanted to see a little more of the world.

Living on an island, almost the only skill that everyone was certain to develop was sailing, or to be more precise, going out on the water. Some of the older islanders sneeringly talked about 'weekend sailors'. There were, it appeared, an increasing number of those who had neither the ability nor the knowledge to use sails as their preferred method of propulsion. Some even eschewed them altogether! Gordon was equally at home with either sails or engines. He had discovered much to his delight that Rhona's uncle – the one who lectured in Gaelic at the Nicolson itself – was as daft on boats as he was himself. As a result the three of them spent many weekends taking Colin McLeod's boat out to sea. By the time Gordon had finished his studies, and was ready to spread his wings, he was an accomplished sailor. Rhona's uncle had said towards the end of their time together, that he felt Gordon could have gone on to become something special, if he had thought of joining the Merchant Navy for example. He was grateful for the confidence shown in his abilities like that, but by then his mind was made up.

While his father was sorry to see his son fly the nest, he recognised the need in the young man to become independent. He was even able to get him an initial placement through some of his own contacts in the hotel business. As a result, Gordon was taken on as an assistant chef in the kitchen of the Duisdale House Hotel overlooking the Sound of Sleat in the South of Skye.

It was his first job, and he was determined to make a success of it. He quickly discovered that the Hotel was a busy one. Set in isolation near to a small beach, it was an attraction for guests who wanted a taste of Scottish Cuisine at its best, while looking at wildlife of every kind from the ground floor panoramic windows. Between hotel guests and the continual influx of those who saw it as a perfect location to start married life and wanted their wedding to be just that little bit different, he didn't have much in the way of spare time. The hotel also boasted its own Yacht – Solus a Chuain – which did a variety of day trips as well as providing a truly exceptional wedding package for the smaller (and wealthier!) groups. It didn't take long for him to be asked if he could act as cook and temporary seaman on occasions there too and, ever ready to expand his CV, he was quick to get involved.

He was well regarded by the management team at the hotel and the wages (and tips!) allowed him to buy a Hansa Liberty – his first boat. It wasn't exactly in the prime of life, but he didn't care – it was his! It enabled him to get out onto the water whenever he had a few hours off. It was just impossible to explain to non-sailors the calming influence of water rushing under your bows as he took the boat out into the Sound and, once or twice, round the northern point of the Isle of Ornsay and out into Loch Houron itself. On one occasion, he had even taken the boat south along the coastline to Sabhal Mòr Ostaig, the Scottish Gaelic College on the Isle of Skye. There, he had had spent a pleasant half hour with a coffee while looking across the water to the Knoydart peninsula, before returning for the evening shift in the hotel kitchens.

It was on one of the wedding trips out on the yacht that he had first met Rachel. She had been taken on as an emergency waitress-cum-dogsbody when one of the regulars had phoned in sick less than a day before the big event. There had been an immediate physical attraction, it was true, but what took her out of the ordinary for him was the soft Welsh accent.

Everyone's efforts were concentrated on making the wedding event something special for the Bride and Groom on each occasion. As the captain had said before they set sail 'the lucky couple are paying well for their big day, it's our job to make them feel it was money well spent'. After the marriage ceremony and speeches had all been made, things quietened down a little on board, but it wasn't until they had disembarked later that Gordon and Rachel found time to talk. Rachel was, apparently, 'bumming around' while she decided what she really wanted to do with her life. She came from Carleon a village on the outskirts of Newport in South Wales. After her 'A' levels had passed – without distinction (she had never been particularly academically minded) – she had started out as a waitress in one of the nearby restaurants. That had given her a bit of money, but not much excitement. Following her nose, and any work that she was able to find, she had been making her way up the west coast of Scotland for some time.

As he went back to his room in the hotel that night, he realised that he wanted to see her again. It hadn't taken long for him to find out that she felt the same way. They could not see each other as much as new couples might. Gordon's hours at the hotel saw to that. It did not take either of them long, though, to feel that what they were becoming involved in was something more than just another short term relationship. When they had eventually sat down and had 'that talk' they discovered that they both wanted much the same things – they both liked the idea of running some kind of restaurant or 'food with accommodation' as she had described it. They both liked boats and were comfortable on the water. When, shortly afterwards, he had sold his Hansa Liberty and bought a 1978 Hallberg-Rassy 31 Monsun, she looked at him with that crooked smile of hers. 'You can't crew that all by yourself, can you?' she asked?

'No, I suppose I can't' He smiled back.

'Did you have anyone in mind to crew with you? she asked.

'You, if you would like to.' He had answered. It was as close as she got to a marriage proposal.

* * * *

12.

'WE REALLY NEED to do something about this before it all gets out of hand – again' said Hilary Watson. 'This' was of course the figures she had handed out to the others at the start of their meeting. They showed that immigrants from the shores of Africa had almost doubled in the last six weeks. Many, but not all of these had entered the country via small boats operating out of a variety of French ports across the Channel.

The increasingly popular route for many of these would-be immigrants was now to travel up through the Bay of Biscay and then berth at one of the channel ports on the French coastline. The French Authorities made no attempts to prevent them doing so, beyond keeping a close eye on them while they were in port, knowing full well that they were merely at a staging point in their journey which would lead across the Channel. Most of them stayed no more than a few days before other, smaller boats came to take them across the Channel and into one of the many coves and sandy beaches which littered the English side of the water.

'We simply do not have the staff to cope with these numbers. Our assessment centres are at breaking point right now. Unless something changes we will have a repeat of those pictures all those years ago of immigrants scaling fences and just walking away into the countryside.'

Graham Oyston took up the argument. 'I've been in touch with all the other European Governments who might be able to help, but there is, as yet, no agreed plan emerging. When I spoke to the French Ambassador here a few days ago he even had the balls to tell me that as we were no longer a 'full' member of the European Community, they were unlikely to make much of an effort to dig us out of a hole. In any case, he said they apparently all have the same thing happening as we do, albeit at a lower level.'

'Why is that?' Eric Mercer asked.

'Why is what?' Hilary responded testily.

'Why are more numbers coming here?'

'Who really knows?' she shot back at him. 'If you want my guess, it's the usual old chestnut that our benefits system gives immigrants, illegal or otherwise, so much more than other Governments have in place. And of course, we are much more welcoming than say, France is. There, they remember only too well the atrocities terrorists carried out in Paris after immigrants had come in illegally to the EU all those years ago, and then vented their venom against innocent French civilians. They are determined that it will not happen again – at least not on their soil. The French attitude has always been a pragmatic one. They apply EU Laws when it suits them and don't where they see a benefit to France in taking that line. As far as immigration goes, they feel that if people want to come here, it is our problem and not theirs, once they have left French soil. They will happily allow them to move to our borders and let them get on their way. I can hardly blame them, can you?'

'So what are you suggesting as a way forward?' Frank Sutherland said. 'I suppose you do have some ideas?'

'Yes' Hilary said. 'Graham and I have already talked it through. As a first step we need to beef up our fleet of coastguard 'screens' along the length of the Channel. If we can intercept these people at sea, we can at least keep them away from just appearing on the mainland. Once we have that under control, we should get the two aircraft carriers that are mothballed in Plymouth up and serviceable as soon as possible. Then we need to get them on station somewhere along our southern coastline – we recommend Portsmouth and Weymouth – and use them as assessment centres. We then make sure that any further boatloads are taken to these ships rather than allowed to dock at any port. Using a facility like that should at least ensure that no-one comes onto dry land until they have been properly processed and we know a little more about them.'

'And how are our 'friends' in the wider EU likely to react to something like that?' Frank asked, turning to the Foreign Secretary.

'We've floated the idea with one or two already' Graham Oyston went on. 'They were, shall we say, rather 'lukewarm' at the idea, but I don't think they will be in too much of a hurry to take us to Court or anything. For a start they are too busy trying to decide what to do about their own problems.

The differences among them we've already seen from our initial chats show that they will take some time to think of what they might want to do about it.'

'As usual with the bureaucrats in the EU, they will take forever whenever a decision is needed. And we, need I remind you, can't afford to wait' Hilary snapped.

'Any thoughts, Eric?' Frank asked.

'I tend to agree with what has already been said' Eric replied, 'but the real reason I'm here is because of the second step in the proposals which Hilary and Graham want to go through.'

'And they are?' Frank said, turning again to The Home and Foreign Secretaries. It was Hilary who led the way again.

'We need to be certain that we can continue to trace these individuals after they have been processed and allowed to go on their way. With the numbers involved and the state of any papers they are likely to have with them, it is a considerable risk that we may be letting potential terrorists in through the gates and then lose them completely as soon as they leave the centres. There will be those who are just immigrants and have little documentary evidence to prove their identities. They are not the problem, or at least they are a simpler problem.

The real problem is the terrorist. They are likely to have contacts already here who can help them to disappear without trace as soon as they are processed. There must be some way of continuing to know where they are. That, I would suggest, is where Eric's scientists are needed.'

'What have you in mind, Eric?' Frank asked.

'Well, you will be aware that we already have the system of tagging for criminals which allows us to monitor their whereabouts once they are released on licence?' The others nodded. 'A slightly more sophisticated system has been in use in the military for some time. There, they have sometimes used a miniaturised form of wristband to ensure they can be picked up quickly by any rescuers when they become detached in battle.'

'So you think we should give our immigrant friends an armband in much the same way?' Frank said, trying to move the discussion along to where decisions needed to be reached – after all he had a meeting scheduled with the American Ambassador in just over an hour.

'That is of course, one possibility' Eric continued. 'However, there are difficulties in using something like a wrist or leg band in this way. They cost money to manufacture and we have only limited stocks so far, enough for our anticipated needs for the erstwhile prisoner usage. There is also the problem that they can be removed – not without effort it has to be said – but it is possible. While that is not a great problem with the criminal element in our society – we can always get hold of them again later, one way or another – we do not want to have the same difficulty with any potential terrorists, do we?'

'So?' Frank asked.

'So, we feel that we should approach this from a different angle. The Army has moved away from the wristband approach for much the same reasons as I've outlined. You will remember the loss of the seven paratroopers in Turkmenistan early last year? That came about because a trap was set where a wristband had been forcibly removed and then used by the other side to become the bait for our prospective rescuers. As a result the Army now uses the latest in our technology. They now use a microchip inserted below the skin in the lower neck which contains a transmitter. Anyone with this inserted can be tracked to within less than a metre.'

'As accurately as that?' Frank said in astonishment.

'Actually, we can now trace the transmitter to within a few millimetres, but when it comes to human sized subjects there is little need for that kind of accuracy. That also has the effect of making manufacture much cheaper as we do not need the higher quality of materials or sophistication in the manufacturing process that the smaller distances require for accurate placement. The transmitters that are being designed right now can actually do a great deal more than that, as well as being somewhat smaller. They were not originally conceived as part of a 'tracing and tracking system' but with minor modifications, they can easily do that job.'

'So' Frank said 'what we are looking at is a way of ensuring, as far as technology can achieve nowadays, that we can track anyone who goes through the assessment centre, find them later and then pick them up if necessary – say when we have more information about them – and deport them if we feel then that there is some kind of specific terrorist risk if they were to remain here?'

'Yes' Hilary said 'and we can have the implant prepared

and inserted as part of the normal medical examination that all immigrants are required to have. We currently use that examination to give them injections against TB and a number of other illnesses that we know are much more prevalent abroad. There is already clear medical evidence that recent upsurges in diagnoses of many of these illnesses among the general British public stem from the last influx of immigrants. There is no reason to feel that this latest influx will be any different and we need to take pre-emptive action on this general disease score anyway. This would just be another item in the syringe.'

'Before we get too far down this road, though' Eric went on 'I need to make you aware of the potential difficulties associated with this approach'.

Hilary sighed loudly and deeply. 'I don't think we need to make too much of possible difficulties right now. We don't even know if the PM here agrees that there is a problem which needs to be addressed'.

'I think I can set your minds at ease on that score' Frank said. 'The figures you've given me today merely put specific numbers against what we all already know and agree is a growing problem, and one that we need to be seen to be tackling. The British public will not thank us if we turn away from taking action to preserve the peace on these islands. They will turn on us at the first available opportunity if they think that we had a way available to us of preventing numbers of terrorists from roaming our streets and did not take appropriate action.'

'Nevertheless' Eric said, over the looks that passed between Hilary and her colleague from the Foreign Office, 'there are difficulties involved if we rush into this without considering all the facts, and I mean *ALL* the facts, not just those that might fit action we've already decided to take.'

Frank Sutherland sat back in his chair. He knew that he would get nowhere with this unless he allowed Eric to have his say. The quicker he let him do that, the quicker he could start to think about the American Ambassador's visit.

13.

THE TALLEST OF the three men had introduced himself as Abdul Rahman as he sat down beside Adisa Folami. The other two remained in the background, stayed standing, and were not introduced. He got the distinct impression that they would only come closer if they saw something that might threaten their patron. Bodyguards were much the same the world over, and Adisa had seen enough over the years to know what the two men were.

Abdul had opened up the discussion by enthusing over Adisa's organisational skills which, he said, had not gone unnoticed elsewhere. He did not elaborate where elsewhere was.

'I have friends who have been impressed by your ability to open up new avenues for our countrymen to reach their chosen destinations. They have many other friends who would like to make a similar journey and take a passage with you.'

Adisa wondered why such a basic ordinary request had led to the man – clearly already well connected if he could afford bodyguards – coming all this way to see him. He had learned over the years that the best way to garner information from people such as Abdul, was to keep quiet. Most of the time the others then continued to talk, at least in part to demonstrate their own importance, and in doing so often said more than was strictly necessary. Information, as always, was one of the most important resources to have.

The plan, when Adisa heard it, was quite unlike anything he had attempted before. When he, and others, had started to look at the Portugal coastline as a possible alternative route to get into mainland Europe, one or two successful trips had been accomplished. Much to everyone's surprise, however, the Portuguese had shown themselves to be remarkably adept at intercepting boatloads of immigrants all along their Atlantic coastline. As a result, those attempting to make the passage into Europe quickly turned their attention to the far north of Spain, beyond the limits of Portugal Authorities, and to try and land some would-be immigrants.

He had already made two successful 'drops' along the largely deserted headland which contained the triple villages of Lira, Larina and Louro. The relatively unpopulated part of Spain there had enabled both the vessel he had used and the immigrants themselves, to operate in reasonable safety. It was one of the longest trips he had undertaken. What Abdul was now asking would be considerably longer.

Abdul said that some of 'his' people were already in mainland Europe, but they wanted to make the onward trip to England. That in itself was not unusual. What he proposed, however, was that Adisa should arrange to pick up his people from roughly the same area in Northern Spain he had already visited, and take them on across the Bay of Biscay and then deposit them somewhere along the Southern Coastline of England. Clearly, from Abdul's explanations, these were not the usual economic migrants he was describing. Adisa was curious as to why people who were already in Europe should want to take further risks just to get to England, but he knew better then to ask questions. He would either get no answer at all, or at best a lie, in response. In those circumstances, he had learned, it was wiser all round if he just kept quiet. As long as they paid well, then it really was none of his business, was it?

The Bay of Biscay was notorious for its dangerous waters and currents, and was not a body of water anyone would attempt – at least not with the size of vessel he had been using for the northern 'run' so far. When he had mentioned this to Abdul, the response had been to talk about the fee that such a venture would command. Adisa could hardly believe his ears. The sum of money would, even after expenses to ship owners and the like, be enough to set him up for life.

There had been the usual bargaining so beloved of all those peoples surrounding the Mediterranean, but both Adisa and Abdul recognised that they were merely indulging in a time honoured tradition which would not affect the actual outcome of the discussions. Abdul had made certain that Adisa was aware that the people would be coming along with several pieces of unspecified equipment.

'It will only be necessary' Abdul had said 'for the boat which picks my people up to be big enough to hold around seven men for the trip out to your larger vessel. I assume that will not be any kind of problem, after all you will be dropping off others as part of the same visit to the shores of Spain. They will not have much to carry, most of what we need will be waiting at our journey's end. Needless to say, no-one else must know of these arrangements. If any Spanish Authorities were to find out about our plans in advance of the trip, they would not be best pleased. That, in turn, would be most unfortunate – for you as well as for me.'

Adisa filed the many questions away in his mind when he heard that. Tonight was not the time to show anything other than agreement. He was, in any case, already starting to think where he might get a vessel which could make this longer trip. If he could combine Abdul's needs with a trip carrying people into Northern Spain, the profits would be enormous, and his mind concentrated on how this could all be coordinated. The meeting had concluded with an agreement that when Adisa had made the necessary arrangements, he would let Abdul know where and when the trip would take place.

* * * *

14.

GARETH THOMAS WAS more than a little disturbed. His two boys, and now Samantha, had been brought up to respect their elders. Whether that was teachers, Nannie or Grandad, or even the village policeman, it made no matter. The phone call from Maddie earlier that afternoon had been a surprise. If what she had said was true, Nathan should not have set up cheek to his teacher Mr Jones. When he parked his van in the driveway, he wondered what he would find when he went in.

Nathan was sitting very quietly on the settee in the front room when he went in. 'What is this all about?' Gareth said. Before Nathan could answer, Maddie came in.

'According to Mrs Wilson the headmistress, he had been rude to Mr Jones' she said.

'What did you say?' Gareth asked Nathan.

'I didn't say anything' Nathan said.

'You must have said something, surely'.

'Mr Jones said that I had hit Arwyn James, and I hadn't.

'And?' Gareth went on.

'And I told him that I hadn't. But he wouldn't believe me.'

'What did happen?'

'Arwyn was being silly, saying that Gavin's mum had been

saying nasty things about him, and Gavin said that wasn't so. Arwyn pushed Gavin and said 'Did so'. Then Gavin pushed him back. I just happened to be standing close to Gavin when he did that, and Mr Jones thought it had been me who pushed Arwyn.'

Maddie said 'I explained all of that to the headmistress, but she seemed to think that I was just making it all up so that Nathan wouldn't get into trouble.'

'So how was it left?' Gareth said.

'Well' Maddie said 'she said that a mark would be entered against Nathan's record, but as it was the first time, no further action would be taken. She did say that she was concerned that the school was getting a reputation locally as a 'rough' place for the kids and she was determined to nip anything like this in the bud. I pointed out to her that, if Nathan was right, there was no need to be concerned about his behaviour. He is, and always has been, a well behaved boy.'

'So should we do anything more about it?' Gareth asked.

'I think it's best to leave it alone' Maddie said. 'It will just continue the argument, and probably make a bigger deal of it than we should. Even then, I might be tempted, but from the way Mrs Wilson, the headmistress, was talking, I don't think we will change anything. We've been getting the same message from our own Headmaster at Ynysddu.'

'OK then' Gareth said 'but if anything like this happens again, I will come with you. No-one is going to level false accusations against my boys. Nathan, you will let Mum or Dad know if anyone at school says anymore about this won't you?'

'Yes Dad' Nathan replied.

* * * *

Adisa had been a little surprised at how easy it had all been to make arrangements. Once he had talked to a few people who knew about the Geography of the North West Spanish area and looked at Google Earth, he quickly settled on a small fairly secluded beach south of the village of Porto de Son. There a road passed within a few metres of the beach and there were only a couple of small houses anywhere in the vicinity. That would enable a relatively safe landing for the refugees he had already started to line up as part of the initial voyage up the coast. They could then be offloaded at the same time as Abdul's men came on board. It would be a simple matter for the larger vessel to remain no more than 1/2 a mile out and wait for the newcomers to arrive. He had found an owner of a ship who was prepared to make the trip.

The M.V. Marianas was an old ship, a long way past its sell by date. The Captain was too. He had struggled, as had many ship owners, to make ends meet these last few years. Constant wars in some of the Mediterranean nations had meant that he could never be sure of a steady stream of work. On one occasion he had accepted a cargo of meat from a cooperative in Greece to be delivered to their agents in Tripoli, only to discover that, by the time he entered the Libyan port, a different Government was in power. By the time he had negotiated his way into, and then out of the port now managed by those directly opposed to the authorities who had placed the original order, the cargo was useless. He had lost a lot of money, money he could ill afford, on that deal. He had, he often reflected, nearly lost his life too. As a consequence, the old man was ready to take on almost any business, especially when Adisa had promised a generous fee and had arranged for half to be paid in advance.

Adisa had envisaged finding a suitable boat to be more of a problem, but the sums of money mentioned had been enough for any reservations on the part of the captain to be swept aside.

15.

As HE STRODE down the corridor towards Meeting Room Three at The Medical Research Laboratory on the outskirts of Godalming, Peter Thomas wondered how the day would pan out. He knew that some of those 'visitors' coming to this meeting wanted to move his research forward. Normally that would have been good news. At the very least, continued funding was like a holy grail to scientists these days, and he knew that this was a distinct possibility given the interest from the politicians he had so recently started to mix with.

Peter's own research was merely a development of Benjamin Forster's work. As is so often the case in scientific research, once the original breakthrough had been made, it opened the floodgates for many others to develop ideas of their own. In Peter's case, he was working with his team to identify more accurately than had ever been possible before, the inter-neuron activity in the brain. How the transfer of information took place and, crucially, what limits there might be to the type and complexity of transfers which they could identify and perhaps modify.

Some of the thoughts he had picked up in those initial discussions with junior political figures and their senior Civil Servants were not so welcome however. The Minister for

Education and Science (his OWN Minister) had indicated when they last spoke, that some of the senior members of the Cabinet had started to take a very real interest in the research results being produced by his team. 'If this continues to be as valuable a tool as some of us are beginning to realise might be the case, there is even the possibility of an award being made' was just one of the many utterances he had heard from Eric Mercer, as his Minister clapped him on the back in some attempt at a false bonhomie.

That was the kind of thing that most people wanted to hear, and scientists were no different. Knowing that their work was well regarded by others. When those others were in positions of influence where they could make things happen, not just talk about them, it became something they would all die for.

Peter knew that more research was required before the work could be safely put into the public domain. There was still so much they didn't know about the interaction between neuron pathways inside the brain. This meeting had come far too early in the research programme for him to be able to give those attending anything really concrete in terms of results. He knew that they would need to be able to evaluate the potential for long term effects (harmful or otherwise) of artificially changing what was happening inside the brain before they could even apply for the necessary licences to allow any of the research to be released for the practical technology which could be expected to follow. Only then could further development begin outside the laboratory environment.

His fears about what others might want to do – and how quickly – had not been quietened by the last conversation he had had with his Head of Research at the Institute. When he had pointed out some of his misgivings, Arnold Patterson had said, in that condescending way he often used, particularly with what he regarded as 'junior' scientists, 'but we all know that more research is always needed, don't we?'

The software programmes he had been developing showed real promise, however. Even Peter had to admit that. When he had started to devise ways of transmitting information at the individual neuron level, others had been quick to spell out the practical difficulties he would have to overcome. It was already known that each neuron could have as many as fifteen thousand connections with other neurons. Even that description was at best only partially correct; because neuron 'connections' did not mean that they were in physical contact with each other. They transfer information when close contact points – called synapses – are active. It wasn't until the advent of the latest computer upgrades that they had had enough power – and speed – to make the necessary calculations to cover most, but still not all, of the possible permutations of this 'contact'.

The revolutionary concept that the gap between neurons and, even more surprisingly, the graded electrical potential between the pre- and post- synaptic neurons, was even more significant in determining the outcome of information transfer than the neurons themselves, had come about slowly. It had not seemed, well, logical. He smiled to himself.

His mother had always hounded him when he was much younger about the amount of time he had spent watching science fiction programmes on their television screen back home in Wales. She had often referred to them, somewhat disparagingly, as 'cowboys and Indians in space'. Even she had recently admitted that it did not seem such a waste of time now.

It had been an utterance from one of his favourite science fiction characters all those years ago, which had helped to put him on the right track. Dr Spock, the coldly logical Vulcan in the vintage series Star Trek, had once said 'when all logical avenues have been explored without success, then whatever remains, no matter how illogical it may seem, must contain the answer'.

Peter and his team of scientists, had spent a long time examining the interaction between neurons, trying to establish how they acted the way they did and why, without coming up with satisfactory answers. When they started to look more closely at the gap between them, they struck gold almost immediately. When the gap was at or less than 1nm – a single nanometre – neurons reacted positively to information fed through them. When the gap was greater than this, the reaction was clearly a negative one. The binding of neurotransmitters to receptors in the postsynaptic neuron can trigger either short term changes, such as changes in the membrane potential which they had started to call postsynaptic potentials, or longer term changes by the activation of what they now termed signalling cascades. Both these changes, short term and long term, could now be seen as either inhibitors or supporters of changes to brain patterns, and through them, changes to individual behaviour.

They were still working on the question of whether the physical distance between the individual neurons, or the electrical potential variation between them, was the main distinction which determined the short or long term nature of the response. They were, however, sufficiently advanced with the other parts of the work to be quite clear that, once that had been fully understood, the rest of the planning for what they were now calling 'the neuron highway' would become just a matter of creating the appropriate mathematical algorithms and a little expert software 'tweaks'.

Those stages were still some way from completion and still had no definitive timescale attached to them. They were all still, to Peter's mind, in the 'research' phase of the work, and not yet ready to see it handed over to the 'technology' end of the business. What had not yet been done (at least to Peter's satisfaction) was make any strides towards identifying what practical uses there might be for the technology or even determining what any real long term effects there might be for individuals who might be tried with the new methods. They were even further from defining whether any changes that they might be able to make, would be of a positive or negative nature.

* * * *

Gordon Morrison and Rachel had spent several months together on the Isle of Skye, before deciding that a move southwards was the right way to try and develop their own dreams. Gordon had been given a glowing reference from the Hotel Management Team, and an even better one from the Yacht owners. When they had sailed over to his Father's establishment in Stornoway to let him know they were heading south, his father had been quick to offer any help he could. He even said that he had a little money put by which he would use to help them to find their own place, whenever they found something to their liking.

Gordon could tell before long that Rachel really wanted to find herself back in Wales. They had touched shore in several places as they went down the West coast of Scotland, but she was always looking for the next trip south. It wasn't until they started to make their way through the Menai Straits that she really perked up. Gordon was very enamoured of the village of Llanfairpwllgwyngll when they berthed for a few days nearby, but in the end they decided that the whole area was far too expensive for anything they could afford. They had come to realise that, while they would in the future depend on tourism for their livelihood, it brought its own difficulties for those who wanted to make their permanent homes in the area. They eventually moved further south round the Llŷn

Peninsula and across Cardigan Bay to Barmouth before they found an area where prices were within their means.

They had struck lucky when they arrived towards the end of the holiday season. Barmouth, like all small holiday resorts, had its fair share of failures amongst the hoteliers each year. Mr. and Mrs. Walters, the elderly couple who had owned and managed the Allt-Yr-Ynys Hotel for more years than either cared to think about, had been through another of the increasingly difficult summers where they had put in a huge amount of work making people happy for too little reward.

As they looked at a bank balance which showed how they were hardly keeping up with the payments they made into their personal pension scheme, they had reluctantly decided that they had worked hard for long enough. No-one was ever going to become a millionaire managing a hotel in the area, and they wanted some leisure in their lives after years of hard work.

What had pushed them into taking that decision was the recent news that their daughter, who lived on the outskirts of Swansea in South Wales, had told them that a first grandchild was on the way. She had gone on to say that it would be nice if the new grandchild should get to know his or her grandparents. When she heard that, Mrs. Walters had looked at her husband and said, 'perhaps someone somewhere is trying to tell us something, don't you think?' He was about to respond with his usual brand of humour which would have led him to say something like 'they're probably trying to tell us they will soon need babysitters' when he looked at his wife's eyes. What he saw there caused him to think again and he just nodded.

With the little bit of money that Gordon's father had promised them, and a little help from the local bank manager, they were able to scrape enough together – just enough – to take over the reins. One of their first acts when they moved in was to change the name of the hotel to the 'Duisdale Hotel' as a memory of where they had first met.

The hotel was not big – twelve rooms – and it was in need of decoration, but it was theirs! Close to the railway station, it was well situated facing the long promenade and sandy beach that were Barmouth's main claim to fame. The little bar inside was one of their best money makers, as tourists who came down to the seafront for the day, as well as those who had rented one of the chalets on the holiday camp at the far end of the promenade, used their hotel as a welcome stop during the long walks that surrounded the area. The harbour was not the best for Gordon's boat, being dry land when the tide was out. He knew he would have to manage the 'wedding' end of his new found business very carefully if he was not to end up with a red face. Weddings on a boat sitting on a sandy harbour bottom were unlikely to bring in much revenue!

Now, a year later, they were fairly well settled into their new environment. The Hotel was making good, if not brilliant, returns and they had no difficulty in keeping their financial head above water. Rachel's idea of booking some 'guest artists' to perform live music in the bar at weekends in the height of the season had been a real money spinner. Within a short space of time it became an attraction for the many families with young children who were the main customers of the chalet site at the far end of the town. Gordon had even felt able to splash out on another boat, this time a Turkish Gulet.

That had been a lucky buy. He had been on the lookout for something that would serve his idea of wedding parties afloat for some time, just like the one run further north at the 'other' Duisdale Hotel. Boats that were big enough to make it a commercially viable enterprise, yet small enough to handle with a crew of perhaps no more than four were not easy to find. The Gulet Furkan 3 had been moored in the Mediterranean but at 24 metres it was about the right size, although, with a top speed of 11 Knots, it wasn't as fleet as he would have liked. Crucially, however, it was at a price he could afford. It could hold up to ten guests and the five bedrooms, done out in mahogany and teak were a dream to see.

One of the consequences of buying a boat that size was that he no longer felt it was a good idea to try and keep it at Barmouth itself. The tidal basin was just too restrictive. Instead he found a mooring further down the coast at Aberdovey where he could get the boat out onto the Bay whenever he needed it. It was a bit further away than he had hoped, but at least he could make use of it whenever a wedding was organised.

There had already been half-a-dozen bookings for weddings on board. He knew that the success of a venture such as this would depend almost entirely on a word of mouth recommendation, and so he was determined that he would make those first few weddings something really special. He might even, he thought, have a chat with the people he knew so well on Skye and see if they could give him a few tips – after all, they weren't going to be in direct competition with each other were they?

* * * *

16.

FRANK SUTHERLAND FELT that the meeting with his three colleagues had gone reasonably well. Even the Home Secretary had seemed relaxed at the end. Was that because he had given in too easily with the proposals she had made, he wondered? Not really, he thought, although you never knew with someone like that. The proposals had been well supported by Graham Oyston and even Eric Mercer hadn't had much to say on the down side of what they wanted to try.

Mercer's objections, such as they were, centred around the usual scientific case that 'more research was needed' before they could be absolutely certain of all the possible side effects. When he had heard that response trotted out elsewhere with remarkable frequency, he had first of all wondered if it was a backhanded way of trying to get more resources for the Minister's Department. He now believed, however, it was more of a defence mechanism that they could remind everyone about later if things went awry.

He had been a little more surprised to hear about the base research which had now been developed into something which had a wider scope for use. The latest developments of the 'Forster chip' as a possible diagnostic tool for treatment of

Alzheimer's was ongoing, as he knew it was. What he hadn't known about was that the research was now showing signs of being really promising in terms of using it to modify patient behaviour in the way Eric had outlined. Eric had been quick to say that they were some way away from getting that to the point where it could leave a laboratory. Eric had also said that was because of the need to pass data on actual symptoms up the line to doctors waiting to translate the information into effective action.

The scientists were currently working on a secure system to ensure that remedial instructions could be fed back down the wireless chain and make significant changes to the neurons most affected by these diseases. Once that could be done consistently, they might have something that could rid the patient of the worst effects of what was known to be a great killer, and then only after the most dreadful periods of suffering that humans had to endure. Frank could tell that, although Eric Mercer had been careful not to mention the word 'cure', that was precisely what was in the wings.

What had been said, however, that was also quite new to Frank, was that the research team was already working alongside scientists who had developed a more sophisticated version of the old GPS technology. One of the drawbacks in making use of any of this work successfully was the fact that doctor and patient needed to be close together for information to be collected and then used. The potential for this research would be enhanced immeasurably if they could make use of it over longer distances than at present. Now,

Frank thought, if that were to become available while he was still in office, he knew he could almost guarantee a successful outcome to the next general election! Presenting a 'cure' for Alzheimer's to the public would be a real feather in his cap. He had indicated as much to Eric.

He had left Eric with the clear view that, if such a breakthrough could be achieved quickly, it would have a positive effect on all their careers. He knew that nothing galvanised a politician more than the thought that they might be able to move up the political ladder. Hilary Watson, on the other hand, had listened to the explanations with a growing sense of excitement. She knew that research was being done in this area, but she hadn't picked up from her own officials that it had reached this stage of development. She was starting to see very quickly where it might become useful in the programme they had all just been discussing. None of the others seemed to be making any connection – yet – but then she knew she was brighter than they were. She had learned that a long time ago.

'Wouldn't it enhance our security immeasurably if we were not only able to keep track of the whereabouts of possible terrorists, but perhaps using this technology that Eric has mentioned, be able to influence their future actions?' she asked.

'Now there's a thought' Graham Oyston added. Eric was about to respond, until Frank decided that it was time to let them all think about that. He didn't have time to listen to any extended explanations, as he still had that Ambassador to see. He did indicate that he wanted to keep an eye on this though, and make sure it was not lost sight of in the other demands made on his time.

He knew that politicians sometimes had to take decisions without all the facts being available to them. If they waited until that happy state of affairs was reached, nothing would ever get done, and he had come into politics to change things hadn't he? No, when all was said and done, it was probably best that they start to do something about the increasing problems being caused almost on a daily basis by the new flood of immigrants coming into Britain from North Africa. They would think about the other aspects just raised after they had sorted out the immediate difficulties.

He also knew that, if they had still been in the EU in all its full majesty, they would never have been allowed the freedom to decide matters like this. The much-vaunted, but increasingly isolated Court of 'Human Rights' would have seen to that. Even the French and German people were starting to raise objections about some of the decisions being handed down from the group of Judges who now sat there. Well paid they were. Elected they were not. And now, as time went on, they were less and less in tune with the needs and desires of the people who paid them. Soon, he felt, they would be disbanded and authority would revert to National Governments.

He felt no real satisfaction at seeing his own long held views becoming a reality. The Courts had caused disharmony within Europe and misery for a considerable number of people who had to listen to them trying to explain some of their decisions. Decisions that to the ordinary man in the street were quite ridiculous and what the legal fraternity would call perverse. The Court was now being seen for what they had been for a long time – a failed attempt at trying to weld a disparate group of nations into one body. Even the most fervent supporter of a 'United State of Europe' had lost patience with them. It was only a matter of time, before they disappeared without trace and, while he couldn't say the words out loud, he felt that such an outcome was not before time.

What he could do was loosen the shackles on the use of this implant and ensure that he had taken all possible options open to him, with the clear priority in mind that it was keeping the citizens of the country as safe as it was possible to do with the technology available. No-one could criticise him for that now, could they?

* * * *

17.

As THE BOAT Yousuf Kanté and his compatriots were in nosed its way past the Faro De Roses and into the small harbour on the far northern border between Spain and France, he realised that he had to find a way of making contact with his mentor Omar Khalil. He had been warned to make no contact until he was certain that there was a very real need to do so. The risks of being caught were just too great. Omar had recognised, however, that at some point in time, such contact would be necessary if the effort put into the whole operation was to be successful. They had always envisaged that Yousuf was a pawn, and no more. A pawn however, which if used properly, could make a real difference in the fight against the terrorism which was still sweeping through the Mediterranean.

As far as the local villagers were concerned, they were just another small boat coming in with a variety of goods, presumably for sale in the local area. There was no reason to think otherwise, as they unloaded the few boxes and other bundles onto the quayside. The decrepit pick-up truck which was waiting for them didn't take long to load men and goods and set off. Half an hour after they had arrived, there was no trace left to let anyone remember that they had ever been there. Even the small boat they had used, moved off within a few minutes of disgorging its load, and – rounding the harbour wall – disappeared shortly thereafter into the gathering dusk. Once the pilot had returned home, he was more busy counting the proceeds from his evening's work than wondering what it was all about. It wasn't often he could make that amount of money just by bringing a few people into harbour from the bigger ship which had paused on it's way to Marseille.

They were taken to a small house nestling at one end of the fairly large, but remarkably empty beach which dwarfed the village itself. After they had eaten, two of the group said they were walking into town to stretch their legs before the journey they would all be making tomorrow. One of them asked Ahmed, their leader, if they could be told where they were heading. He said, 'I suppose there is no harm in telling you now that we are well on our way. We are travelling to the Atlantic coast tomorrow and then we are taking a sea trip to wreak havoc amongst the little Satan.' They all knew that they were talking about the Hated English when he used that description. The Great Satan was, of course America.

Yousuf knew that was information which would justify the risk in trying to make contact. He stood up and said he needed exercise too, but would head out towards the other end of the beach.

'Maybe there will be something other than a lady of light love to interest me there' he said. The rest greeted that thought with hoots of laughter.

It was easy to check, as he walked along the beach front, that no-one from the house came after him. All he needed was a phone booth and he quickly found one a little way down a dingy side street. Tourists, who made up the majority of people on the streets at this time in the evening, were not likely to venture down such an out of the way area, and so he felt quite safe. The telephone number he needed was already burned into his memory. The code words he could choose from were not many, but enough to alert Omar that he was now moving in a way which indicated that some kind of attack was going to be made somewhere in England, and relatively soon.

He had always been very careful about what he carried when out with this group of people. He knew that his life depended on them not being able to tie him into anything which was in the least bit unusual for a soldier of Islam to be carrying. It was however, obvious that they were planning something big, and so he had to find ways of keeping in contact to make sure he could pass on information before they could do whatever they intended. He carried a knife at all times, but then so did everyone else.

As he walked away from the phone booth, he saw a shop advertising mobile phones. He didn't hesitate. There was little risk, he reckoned, in having one of those. Most people did nowadays, although he had only seen Ahmed using one within the group. However, the shop keeper had been quick to point out this one was one of the cheaper models. Even at this basic level, it had many features that he neither needed nor would ever use. It was capable of receiving its signals from satellite rather than any land based transmitter and even had a facility for sending a signal to anyone who knew the number he was using, telling them where in the world the signal was coming from, and therefore where he was.

The shopkeeper explained that it was very similar in essence to the 'black boxes' which commercial airliners carried to enable them to be found and the data they contained to be analysed even if they and the aeroplane they were in were both at the bottom of one of the oceans. The one built into the phone was of course much smaller in size, merely the size of a small microchip, but it fulfilled the same function. That, he felt, might turn out to be a very useful feature. Older versions needed to be within reach of a land-based transmitter and he now knew that where he was going would not allow that to happen.

He knew he would not be able to charge it up openly, but the shop owner had assured him that it was already fully charged. It would, he said, last for several days if he switched it off when not using it. If the worst came to the worst he could explain that he had just wanted to see what games they had on it without him needing to spend a lot of money on what was otherwise a fairly useless toy. They all knew he had no immediate family, although none of them knew the true story of how that had come about.

18.

THE MEETING HAD started badly for Peter Thomas. He knew that. There were representatives from a variety of Government Departments in attendance to hear about his research. Each of the interested Departments had sent along one of their Scientists as well as one of their senior administrative staff to hear what he had to say. As soon as the Chairman had opened the proceedings and immediately congratulated him and his work, he had gone on to say he was sure that – while they would all recognise the work that still needed to be done – it was already showing great promise for use in the practical world they all lived in. Peter could sense that it was going to go wrong. After giving a short introduction to the work so far done, he had started to point out the work that was still needed, but he could sense that a number of listeners 'switched off'. He was being listened to, but not understood.

There were not many questions at the end. One or two of the scientists asked fairly esoteric questions which showed just how specialised his own research had, of necessity, become. They, at least, wanted to know more. The non-scientists were much more guarded in their questioning. What questions did come from them centred mainly around the effectiveness of information transfer between Neurons, and the ways in which it could be delivered to a number of 'subjects' at the same time. He didn't have answers to some of that, but he felt he was unable to get them to fully understand the difficulties in transferring the theoretical models they had already completed into something that could be applied in the 'real' world. He was left with a strange sensation that they wanted to continue their deliberations somewhere else.

There was, he realised quite quickly, another agenda being followed by some of the people in the room. He did get one or two smiles of sympathy from the other scientists there, but they were well hidden from their political masters in the other Departments represented at the meeting.

As he left the meeting at the end, he wondered what it had all achieved. He had hoped for a greater degree of understanding about some of the difficulties he still faced, but he realised that, no matter how senior some of those attending might have been, they were still admin types, and couldn't be expected to understand the scientific problems fully.

He wasn't the type to bury his head in the sand, however, and so next morning he knocked on Arnold Patterson's door and went in.

'Come in, come in' Arnold said with a broad smile. 'That went quite well, yesterday, don't you think'?

'Actually I didn't' Peter responded.

'Really! Why ever not?' Was the reply.

'Well, I got the distinct impression that other agendas were present, or have I got that all wrong?'

Arnold sat back and looked at Peter. 'I wouldn't call them other 'Agendas' Peter' he replied. 'It's just that our political masters have different imperatives than, perhaps, a pure scientist such as you or I might have. Most of the Civil Servants who were listening to you yesterday are very close to their ministers and will have come with the specific brief to extract as much political capital from what you had to say as was possible. The politicians are always mindful that they are being watched by the media in particular, to ensure that they do not stray too far from election promises and pledges that they might – no, make that will – have made in the past. None of them want to see their names up in lights in the Tabloid Media, as it were, because of some failure to take on board advances which might prove beneficial to society. The additional factor is, of course, that they all work to a different time frame to ours. Theirs is bounded by the date of the next General Election, while we have a more measured approach to our work don't we?

'There is no point in seeing 'reds under the bed' in a situation like yesterday. It is merely the way things often work. As you move further into these kind of meetings when discussing research, you will have to realise that the political side of the equation sometimes takes over from the more cautious and meticulous approach that we try and adopt.'

'Does this mean that there is nothing you – or I – can do to influence them?'

'No, I wouldn't put it quite like that. We know where there are still significant 'holes' in the research, don't we? Well we must just push for these to be recognised by our political masters and hope that they realise the potential problems they could unleash if they move too fast'.

* * * *

One of the consequences of the decision to move his allegiance to the Free Church meant that Donald McLeod had to vacate the Manse that had been his residence as Minister of the Church of Scotland. While he and Colin had become more in tune with one another, he had declined the somewhat strained offer from his brother to move in with him – at least on a temporary basis. Instead, he moved back into the family home where his mother welcomed him like the prodigal son of the Bible. Their father had died several years ago, succumbing to Pneumonia one winter's night, and she was glad of the new, if unexpected, company.

James McMillan, the Minister of the Free Church in Stornoway, while welcoming the new increase in parishioners, had made it plain privately to Donald that he did not expect to see him become a 'Minister-in-Waiting', or anything like that. That suited Donald fine. He had no intention of rocking any boats in that direction, but as he had said to James 'we are coming into your congregation, because we believe it mirrors our own approach to the scriptures and how we should live our lives. As long as that approach does not change, you will get no problems from me. I cannot, however speak for the rest. They are God fearing people, and adults who can make their own minds up. I am not, and will never be their leader, but I will not stay quiet if you stray from the paths that we both know to be the right way.'

19.

Bryn Thomas had always wanted to be in control of his life from as far back as he could remember. He had been farmed out to a variety of childminders throughout his early years. They had changed frequently as his parents looked for the cheapest way of having him cared for before he went to school. Then a variety of others had appeared on the scene as his parents felt the desire to have 'free time' unencumbered by a child tagging along as they enjoyed themselves each weekend. At that time in his life, he had no control over what happened. He could do nothing except accept that this was what life – his life – was like.

He had, however, made sure that, when he had his own family, he would be with them as much as possible. That way he would always be around when decisions needed to be taken about their welfare. He and Sally had laughed occasionally about how she wasn't allowed to make any decisions when he was around. When she was pregnant, he made sure that he was there at any meetings with nurses or doctors to discuss the needs of his wife. He was oblivious to the rolling eyes which became the norm as the pregnancy developed and his input became ever more vociferous. He made sure that things were going to be done as he wanted.

He wanted his boys to have the best of everything. He well remembered some of the hand-me-downs his own parents had given him. His first bike had been one that was on its last legs, having been ridden into the ground by his cousin Jamie before his parents had taken it over. His Dad, prompted by his Mum, had at least reluctantly tried to paint it so that some of the rust would not be too obvious. But his dad had been a mechanic, not a painter. His Mum had noticed how he had reacted to that. His Dad was completely oblivious, as always.

Later on when he moved into a business partnership with his Dad, he had long arguments with the old man about how they should build the business. His father just wanted to keep things as simple as they had always been. It led to a quieter life that way and didn't interfere with his leisure time in any way. Bryn, however, wanted more. He saw the possibility of expanding the firm until it could be seen as a quality enterprise by the whole area. That way, he could see the profits increase ten fold. He could almost smell the money when he had started to move into the second hand car market, often selling them on at immense profit.

Those long ago arguments had defined the relationship of father and son for the rest of their lives. Bryn had the ideas, but his father didn't want to get involved. They argued until the old man said something along the lines of 'have it your own way, just don't expect me to sweat out extra hours to give you more money'. Bryn then did what he wanted and kept his old man out of it. Eventually they stopped having the arguments, and Bryn just did what he wanted. As Bryn reflected many a time however, the old man was quite content to accept the extra monies in his monthly 'take' from the business. Bryn didn't really object to those arrangements. His father got an easy life, he got total control.

Control – of everything and everybody in his life – became an unconscious but very real need for him. Without it he could not function properly. When Sally had left some years ago, he was more angry than sad. Angry that she would not listen to what he wanted to do, and angry that he could no longer control her in the way he had become accustomed to doing. It was almost too much to bear when he discovered that she was staying no more than few miles away. She still wanted to keep in touch with Gareth and Peter – HIS boys – and he would not stand for that. She had left and so he was going to make sure she left – completely. Cutting the 'deal' with her over a divorce settlement had cost him a lot of money, but it was money well spent in his eyes to make sure that he kept the boys and she kept away from them all. He was still, even after all this time, annoyed that Peter had left as soon as he could and was now living somewhere in the South of England close to where Sally lived with some new man. He knew she would never marry again – that had been part of the deal.

When it became apparent that Gareth was becoming more assertive in what needed to be done with the business, they had had several rows. It was only when Gareth had threatened to leave and set up in competition with him that he relented. He still felt that Maddie had been behind Gareth and those rows. Gareth had always been too timid to offer any real opposition to Bryn's orders – until he had married.

Although he would never have admitted it to anyone, he had felt the need to fill what was slowly becoming a rather empty and lonely life. Entering politics at the local level in Newport would, he believed, have helped, but in the event it had been something of a shock to Bryn. He had never been what you might call a 'political' animal. His involvement had largely come about because he saw it as an easy way to meet people of all kinds, some, if not most of whom, he felt he could 'do a deal' with in relation to his business.

He had fondly imagined that his new Chairmanship of the Local Government Education Committee would involve making decisions that others would have to abide by. What he had not expected was the constraints that budgets would put on his – and other Councillors – ability to do more or less what they wanted. He had argued in Council for increases in funding, but had little support from the other Committee chairmen, all of whom were fighting for money out of the same small and ever decreasing 'pot'. Having to juggle funds even within his own little empire was not something he had expected. He had done enough of that when he was in full control of the family business.

Here, though, he couldn't just decide and then let others get on with it. Here, he had to persuade others on the Committee that what he wanted to spend money on was the right priority. He also had to defend the whole Education department against criticisms from Central Government about the performance of most of the schools in the area. There were dire warnings of the financial consequences for his future budgets if things didn't improve – and soon.

Behaviour of pupils, particularly in the primary years, was a constant theme of the criticisms. He knew he was going to have to do something about that. Something that wasn't going to cost a lot of money.

20.

WHEN YOUSUF KANTÉ awoke, it took him a few moments to realise where he was. It was only when he felt the soft rolling of the ship that it all came flooding back to him. He wondered if this journey on the M.V. Marianas was going to finally bring him to the end of the journey which had started all those years ago in Cairo.

The trip across northern Spain had been tiring, but unremarkable. An old and fairly decrepit transit van with seven men in it was also quite unremarkable for the area. He had been surprised at just how unpopulated the whole area had been. The southern foothills of the Pyrenees seemed to consist of nothing more than a succession of small villages with large distances between them.

That was good for their purpose. The fewer people there were around, the less chance of someone noticing and perhaps then asking awkward questions, but he had time to wonder how the locals managed to scratch a living out of the soil. It was not the most fertile of places to either grow crops or even feed livestock. He saw little evidence of either out of the window he was pressed up against throughout the two day trip.

The small town of Vitoria-Gastiez was almost the mid

point of their journey, but no-one paid any attention to the group of dishevelled and weary men who had decamped at the run-down house on its southern outskirts. Someone had obviously gone to a great deal of trouble to make sure that there was enough food and bedding to give them all a good night's rest. There was no question of any of them going outside – that would have been far too likely to have led to someone noticing the group of men who were all strangers to the area. As a result they settled back after their meagre meal and, as men do in these situations, chatted away among themselves.

Most of them were quiet types, not given to casual chit chat. The business they were embarking on also had a sobering effect on them as they came nearer and nearer to their objective. Rifat Tawil, however, had known Ahmed Chisisi before this operation and was always glad to show the others how friendly he was with the leader of the group. He clearly felt it gave him a status denied the others.

'This has been one of our easier operations so far Ahmed' he said. 'Do you remember the time I had to smuggle in those two vests ready rigged with explosives for our soldiers to use in Cairo? The one which was used in the Café frequented by the police was followed quickly by the one used in the Mosque. Remember the one on the road into the City from the Airport? That took some organising. It was a shame that our soldiers could not return from those efforts, but they knew they were doing Allah's work, just as we are now.' Ahmed smiled and replied 'it is true that Allah has smiled on our work so far. Pray that he will continue to do so.'

Yousuf froze as he heard the dialogue between the two men. Omar had been correct when he said that he had information linking Chisisi to the Mosque bombing so long ago. Now he knew another member of the group who had been involved in that atrocity. He would not forget this conversation. Although Rifat Tawil did not yet know it, he had just signed his own death warrant. From now on, he was another target.

No-one paid any attention when the group left the next morning either. It was late evening on the second day of their travels when they pulled into a lay-by just over 1/2 a mile south of the town of Porto de Son on Spain's Atlantic coast. Ahmed immediately left the van and walked a little way towards the beach. There, Yousuf could see him talking on his telephone. When he returned, Ahmed announced that they would be spending the night sleeping in the van. The next day they would relax; perhaps even take a dip in the waters of the Playa de Fonforron – the beach area immediately to their north. They had brought food with them to cover this eventuality, and would cook it here. The path down to the beach itself provided adequate cover for this to be done without drawing undue attention to themselves. Ahmed said it would be unwise to let the locals see a group of unknown men come into their village, even if only for a snack. They would then, he said, be fully rested for the next part of the trip. A boat would be arriving offshore on the next night and they would then begin the final leg of their journey.

Yousuf knew that he had somehow to take advantage of this break in travelling to alert Omar about the plans as he now knew them. If they were to make the last leg of the trip on board a ship, he didn't know if he would be able to do anything then without being seen or overheard. They made a small fire on the slope leading from the lay-by down to the rocks above the beach where they would be leaving later. After eating, the group split up and did their own thing throughout the day. Some went down to the waters edge, while others made their way over the road away from the beach area to where trees provided cover from prying eyes. Any local who passed would not be able to see them as they relieved themselves amongst the trees there.

It was mid afternoon when Yousuf felt the need, and decided to make the same journey. He hefted the small shovel they had all been using, and went up the hill on the other side of the road. Disappearing into the trees, it was a moments work to dig the small hole and then as he squatted he pulled out the mobile phone he had guarded so carefully. It took only a moment for him to be connected to the voice back in Cairo who answered 'Omar'.

'I have acquired a phone, make note of this number and keep track of where it is. That is where I will be. I may not get the chance to make voice contact with you for some time. We are going by boat from here tonight and heading towards England, but I do not as yet know our precise destination, or what is being planned when we get there.'

'I am sure it will be some kind of fresh attack which

they hope will make headlines across the world' Omar said. 'It is now our job to do what we can to stop it, if we can. I will contact my friends in England and alert them to what is coming. Do you know the name of the ship you are to board?'

'No' Yousuf replied.

'Try and find this out, if you can. It would also be extremely useful if we can know in good time where the boat is to drop you and the others off. That will make it much easier to arrange a welcoming committee.'

'I will try' was all Yousuf had to say.

As he turned the phone off, he was aware of a noise from behind him. Turning, he saw Rifat Tawil looking over at him in disbelief. Yousuf just had time to pull his trousers up before Rifat turned to run away. Yusuf could see all his time and plans being lost in that instant. It was almost a reflex action, but his earlier training in the police gave accuracy to his actions. He pulled out the knife he carried and threw it. He had not forgotten the fact that this man had played a large part in his family's deaths, and so he put all his strength into that throw. When the knife struck it did so with such force that it almost severed Rifat's head from his shoulders. The man dropped silently to the ground as his blood spurted everywhere.

Yousuf was aghast. Not at the killing. He had already seen and done too much of that for it to affect him. He had already accepted the fact that he was going to die as an inevitable part of this operation, and saw no good reason why any of the others should outlive him. However, if his efforts were to be successful, he was now aware that he had an immediate problem to deal with. How did he conceal the body until such time as they all left later that night?

Looking around, he saw that there was the usual undergrowth you would expect from this kind of terrain. Dead branches, and other smaller bushes abounded. He needed something more. Then a few yards away he saw a group of large boulders, possibly left there after the nearby road had been improved. They were overgrown with weeds but, he could see, were spaced in such a way that, with a few of the larger branches already laying around, a makeshift hiding place was possible. It wouldn't stand up to close scrutiny, but then perhaps it didn't need to. They would not be easy to move, but he could bring the body over to them and perhaps use the smaller branches to provide more cover. It was not brilliant, but it would have to do. After all, he reasoned, it only had to provide cover for a few hours. Then they would all be on their way, never to return.

Fifteen minutes later he was on his way back to the group. No-one paid any attention as he put the shovel back where it was kept and then squatted back down beside the van.

It was over three hours later, and getting grey dark when Ahmed Chisisi said 'has anyone seen Rifat recently?' No one had and, after a pause, Yousuf felt bold enough to say 'I thought I saw him head off down to the beach, but that was some long time ago.' Ahmed shrugged and said 'I hope he gets back soon. I don't want to have to leave him here.'

One of the others said 'perhaps he has found a mermaid and has gone out to sea with her.' They all laughed. A little later Ahmed said to a couple of the others 'have a walk down to the beach will you? It's just possible that he has hurt himself or something, and we should get him back here now if we can.'

Yousuf could see that Ahmed might just try and spread the net a little wider, and so he said 'would you like me to take a walk over to where we were all using the shovel? Perhaps he has gone there and injured himself. At least we can then rule that area out, if you're still concerned.' Ahmed nodded to him. When they all returned some minutes later with the news that Rifat was nowhere to be seen, Ahmed was not a happy man.

'How can he have disappeared' he demanded of no-one in particular. One of the others said 'perhaps he changed his mind, perhaps he has decided to work for the other side.' Ahmed turned on him furiously 'I have known Rifat since we were children, brought up in the same part of Baghdad. There is no way he has walked away from us and his part in attacking our enemies. Something must have happened.' One of the others said truculently 'what can we do about it? What can you do about it? We can't find him, and we don't have the time to send out more search parties.' Ahmed turned and stalked away. He wasn't happy, but he knew the man was right.

Some three hours later, as the remaining six men climbed up the ladder and into the M.V.Marianas which had so recently disgorged its human cargo of would-be immigrants ready to find a new life on mainland Spain, there was still no sign of Rifat. Ahmed spent most of the time on the short trip to the vessel moored offshore, looking back at the beach in a vain attempt to catch sight of his oldest friend.

* * * *

21.

WHEN PETER THOMAS came out of the meeting chaired by his Head of Research and the Minister Eric Mercer several hours later, he knew he had to talk to someone – someone well outside the rarefied atmosphere he had just been in.

There had been a 'full house' of Government Ministers at the meeting. Not only was Eric Mercer there as Head of the Department for Education and Science, but also a Martin Cook had been introduced to those who didn't know him. Martin was apparently the Minister with specific responsibilities for schools in what was a fairly new reorganisation of Government Departments. The joining together of Science and Education into a joint Ministry had only taken place some five years ago, and they were already on their third Minister for Schools. Martin had not said a word during the sometimes heated exchanges, presumably because he was still getting the feel for his own responsibilities.

Peter could still hardly believe what he had heard. He had already had his reservations about what might be said, but even in his worst nightmare, he had not envisaged anything quite like what he had so recently heard and argued vehemently and unsuccessfully against. His own Minister had even put him down on one occasion, telling him that the areas he was straying into with his objections were the province of politicians – elected by the people, he had archly said – rather than those of a scientist employed by Her Majesty's Government.

As the small group filed silently out afterwards, he was approached by one of the other men who had attended the meeting. Introducing himself as Geoffrey Williams, he said, with some distaste, 'it looks as if those in authority are going to take this research of yours in hand and try and make something very big out of it. They obviously see a great deal of political capital out of moving this forward as quickly as they can. Did you notice that Martin Cook never said one word during that meeting?' Peter said he had. 'But did you also see the amount of note-taking he was doing? You mark my words; we have not seen the last of him or his underlings.'

When Peter had protested again at the speed with which things seemed to be moving, Geoffrey had responded 'I know only too well what can happen when our political masters get an idea in their heads. Perhaps we should have a coffee in what passes for a canteen in this place and I can fill you in on what I've been doing, and what some of the outcomes have been. It looks to me as if they will try and marry your work on information transfer and messaging at the neuron level to my work on SPPS. We may well find that we will be starting to work much more closely together.'

* * * *

While the two scientists were outlining their views and fears for what the future might have in store for Peter's research, Eric Mercer was listening to his Head of Research, Arnold Patterson, explaining that it might not ever be possible to link SPPS technology with the research being done by Peter Thomas in quite the way he wanted. The idea of not only finding out where Immigrants actually were, but being able to use the Neuron Highway to get them to voluntarily come back to the Immigration Authorities was really pie in the sky as far as present research went.

Arnold was trying to explain in greater detail than had been possible in the meeting how he saw the present position of Peter's research.

'You see Minister, Peter's development work based on the 'Forster Chip' has been an excellent piece of work,'

'I'm well aware of that.'

'It is also within very strictly defined and rigid parameters and in a very limited response range. What you have just been outlining goes much further than that. I have no doubt that Geoffrey Williams' work will enable potential terrorists' movements to be tracked quite precisely. I am also quite confident that Peter will soon be able to programme the miniaturised implant in such a way as to deliver messages to the 'subject.'

'Quite' Mercer said somewhat testily. 'So where do you feel there is some problem then? I assume that you do see a problem?'

'What Peter is still far from being able to do, is ensure

that instructions delivered in the way now being discussed would lead to a response which could be assessed and then modified to get the subject to exhibit a satisfactory level of understanding and change in behaviour. It is a little like the difference between telling the subject to 'go home', or telling them to call into the supermarket and having them bring back specific items of shopping on the way. In terms of the electronic transfer of information and instructions, the first was a relatively simple programming exercise while the second was exceedingly complex.'

Eric Mercer let Arnold have his say for a while, before interrupting him. 'But from what I've heard so far, Peter and his team are able to get information from a subject using this 'Neuron Highway', I think he calls it, can't he?'

'Yes, that is true Minister, but...'

'And from what I've gleaned from some of my own people who were at that other seminar recently, he is able to use that information and then translate it into some kind of response which can be sent back down the line and will affect the subject's subsequent behaviour, isn't he?'

'Yes, Minister, but...'

'Well I don't see that what I'm suggesting is so very different in essence from what he is already doing, is it?'

'The big difference is that you are suggesting that it should be done outside laboratory conditions before we have validated the consistency of responses we are able to obtain. We simply don't know enough about the range of responses we might get and what they might mean as yet. In the laboratory we can see and assess these properly before we 'go live' as it were.'

'Let me come at this from a different direction then, Arnold. Before any piece of research is properly validated, it needs to be used – trialled if you will – in the real world, doesn't it?'

'Yes, Minister, but...'

'All I'm really saying therefore is that it is necessary to speed up the normal process a little in order to meet difficulties the Government faces in dealing with this latest immigration issue. It would be utterly pointless to have such a facility on the point of use and not at least try it out 'in the field' in order to help solve a real difficulty. We need to make use of this piece of science, and we need to make use of it now, not in six months or perhaps a year from now. It could all be too late by then. Don't you agree?'

'Yes Minister.'

'Then kindly put the wheels in motion. This piece of work is arguably the most important area that the station is involved in right now, and it should receive the most attention if we are not to 'miss the boat' quite literally. We can have another chat about progress on this when we next meet at our regular monthly get together, Ok?'

Arnold was more than a little taken aback to hear his Minister say that the research in this area was now to be accorded top priority, even to the extent that funds already earmarked for other areas were to be shifted over to this work. He was even more alarmed to hear Eric Mercer say that failure to come up with meaningful results like this when required, could have a serious effect on future funding for the whole station. The final statement that they would meet on a monthly basis from now on with the specific topic of ensuring that adequate progress was being made, made Arnold wonder what really had caused such a change in priorities for a man who, until now had seemed quite an amenable Minister. He might even have been wrong, he thought, as he drove home later that night, when he had said to Peter Thomas that there were no hidden agendas at work. If there were, he would have to try and find out what they were.

* * * *

Later that evening as Peter made his way back to the flat he shared with Rhona McLeod, his girlfriend of more than five years, he wondered what the next few months might bring. Even more importantly, he wondered how he felt he was likely to react to whatever lay ahead. Geoffrey Williams was clearly much more experienced than he was in dealings with the whole government machine. Peter had already known that the SPPS technology had been the basis for Williams' Nobel Prize. What he hadn't been aware of was the way it was now being used in the Army and would shortly be used in relation to the prison service.

When he had described to Peter the possibilities for this new technology once it was wedded to Peter's own research into Neuron Information Transfer, it had not made for a pleasant conversation. He had always seen the real value of his work as being in the medical field where he could make a difference to the quality of life for those who suffered from the diseases of old age. After talking to Geoffrey, and hearing how his work on SPPS had been changed markedly at the behest of their political masters, he was beginning to realise just how naive he may have been. He knew he had to seek out some more views to help him in assessing what might be the best way to deal with what increasingly seemed to be a difficult way forward.

He had always been the 'bright spark' in the family. The one who was quickest, both in his understanding of any question put to him at school, and his ability to have a cheeky answer if he thought it would get a laugh from classmates – especially the girls. When it came to looking at things in a more considered way, however, he had always relied on his elder brother Gareth to think things through before he opened his mouth. He regretted that circumstances had created a distance between them, but always knew that he could rely on his older brother to provide a more reasoned and rational view when thorny problems came up. Gareth was the one he needed to speak to now.

When he told Rhona of his concerns, she was quick to agree that a trip home to the valleys of South Wales was a good idea. She had only visited Peter's brother and father twice since she had become Peter's girlfriend and partner, but she too saw a solid calming influence on Peter when he was in the company of his older brother. When she had first come into contact with the younger brother while they were both studying Biology at Southampton, she had been entranced with his ready wit and intellect. That had only grown stronger as time had passed, but her own upbringing on the Isle of Lewis in the Outer Hebrides had given her that unique ability to see at least a little of what was inside a person, rather than stop at the surface image they presented to the world.

Gareth, to her eyes, was so similar to many of the men folk in her own far north-west. Quiet and softly spoken much of the time, they had an inner strength which had always been so attractive to her, and she guessed, most women. Like those from her own homeland, she was prepared to believe that Gareth would be someone you would always want by your side rather than facing you, when things got tough.

22.

WHEN JAMES MCMILLAN had been asked to speak at the next ICRC – The International Conference of Reformed Churches – he had been proud to accept. Not proud for himself, of course. Pride was considered to be at best unseemly for a Minister of his Church, and at worst something of a sin. No, he was proud that his church had been recognised by others in the Movement as worthy of having views which needed to be listened to, before making decisions on the way to move forward. These invitations were not given out lightly, and as each Conference was held only once in four years, they were prepared very thoroughly and well in advance. He had not realised at the time he had accepted the invitation, that his wife was going to be due to deliver his first-born at the same time as he was supposed to be speaking at the upcoming Conference.

He was supposed to speak against the motion attempting to recognise wider sexual relationships within the family marriage, than the one handed down in God's word. It was complete anathema to him, and most others in his Free Church Of Scotland Reformed Church. In his view, the Bible was quite explicit on the issue. He knew that while there were other Churches within the Reformed umbrella who agreed with his stance, there were also others, and a growing number at that, who did not. Putting his point of view forward, and having it accepted was not only important from a personal perspective, it was crucial from the wider Church point of view.

He knew that the subject matter was likely to be critical for the continuation of the Free Church of Scotland's membership of the bigger Movement. Speaking to most other congregations across Scotland in the last few years, it was obvious that if their views did not win the day, there was almost certainly going to be a strong desire for the Church to leave the Movement altogether. He understood those feelings only too well, and to a great degree shared them. He had, however, seen for himself some of the benefits that belonging to a bigger group with far flung contacts across the world had brought. They had all benefitted, he thought, from exposure to different perspectives which had come from as far afield as Korea and Africa.

Mission work had always been one of his passions. Bringing the word of God to others who had known no God beforehand was something that he felt was, and should be, at the very core of the Church's belief and work. It was even enshrined in The Canons of Dordrecht – one of the three Forms of Unity which bound their whole Movements together. There it says:

Article 3: The Preaching of the Gospel
In order that people may be brought to faith, God

mercifully sends proclaimers of this very joyful message to the people he wishes and at the time he wishes. By this ministry people are called to repentance and faith in Christ crucified. For how shall they believe in him of whom they have not heard? And how shall they hear without someone preaching? And how shall they preach unless they have been sent?

(Rom. 10:14-15).

Leaving the Movement would bring such involvement to an abrupt end, and he was determined to do all that he could to ensure this would not be the outcome of the debate.

When he had decided to speak to Donald McLeod, he knew that he had to be careful with his words. Although, he had come to like the rather abrasive Islander, he realised that Donald was someone who had very clear and firm views on what was appropriate for the Ministry. When discussions took place within the church, he did not hold back. It was a little surprising to notice the different approach to almost every area of church work that the two brothers exhibited. Colin was a gentle man, as well as a gentleman. Donald, on the other hand, saw only retribution and eventual damnation for those who didn't see things his way. There were, as a result, very real difficulties in seeking his help like this.

Donald could easily be so dogmatic, failing sometimes to even want to see any other perspective than his own. James had real concerns that Donald could lose the debate simply because of the way he presented the arguments, rather than because of the logic he might bring forward. On balance, however, he felt that Donald's powerful oratory, if it could be harnessed properly, had a very good chance of winning the day. Nothing was without risk, he knew, but in this case, he felt it was a risk worth taking.

He approached Donald after the Sunday service and asked if he would come round to the Manse that evening when the service was over. Donald explained that Colin usually came over to see their mother on a Sunday evening, and they spent some time together then. James said that he had been thinking of having a chat to Colin on much the same subject and might it be possible to see them together? Donald said that they would both come over as soon as they had finished their evening meal.

It was around eight o'clock that the Manse doorbell rang. Opening it, James found both brothers standing on the doorstep. Colin said 'this had better be good James. Mother is all agog at what might occasion us having to come out at this time of night on the Sabbath.'

'I need your help – both of you.'

'Fire away then James' Donald said as he settled down in one of the armchairs in the large front room. James waited until his wife had brought in the inevitable cup of tea for them and then left them to get on with it.

When James had finished outlining his difficulty over the timing of both the Conference and his wife's forthcoming confinement, he sat back.

'Well' Donald said. 'To say that this is unfortunate does

not do the situation justice. We both know that we will need a strong speaker on that subject at the Conference. You do realise, don't you, that unless a consensus is reached which matches our views up here, we will have some very serious decisions to make? I need not remind you, that it was precisely this issue which led to us joining this congregation all those years ago?'

'Yes' James replied, 'in fact it is because of that, that I feel you would be the best person to give a view on these issues to the Conference in my stead.'

'I know you have a sense of humour, James' Colin joined in, 'but I must say that this is something that we – all of us – shouldn't joke about.'

'I agree completely, Colin, but why should you think that I would want to joke at this time?'

'Well, you cannot really be serious that Donald should represent the views of the whole Church on this, surely' Colin went on.

'Oh, but I am.' James said. 'I've talked to both the Conference organisers and several of the other ministers in our faith. They all agree that I have to find a replacement. The Conference organisers said that they still wanted to hear from our own Church in Scotland on this topic. They know it has been long debated here with strong views being put forward on both sides of the argument.

'When I mentioned Donald's name to our own Church members, they agreed that this was the best way to ensure that we – they – have their views properly represented. He may not have his own Church to care for, but your service on some of our major committees has meant that both of you are not only well known throughout our wider Church, but are respected for your views. He has clearly shown – you both have – that you have the interests of our faith well to the fore in everything you say or do. I may not always agree with some of the things Donald expresses, but I would never question either his sincerity or his abilities to get a message over.'

The two brothers looked at each other.

'If – and it is still a big 'if' – I agree to this idea of yours, I must insist on doing it my way' Donald said. 'I will not be prepared to approach this from any other viewpoint than my own. I'm not sure I would be capable of doing anything else, and in any case, I feel that to try would be dishonest of me.'

'I've discussed this with others around our broad church before I asked you to come here tonight' James said. 'I had a feeling that you would say something like that.' They all smiled.

'And?' Donald pressed.

'And they are more than ready to accept that you should say your piece from the heart. They have heard you both on this subject on more than one occasion in the past, and they are content that you should repeat those views in any way you feel the occasion needs.'

'Well, Donald' Colin said. 'It looks like you're elected.' Turning to James, he said 'Why did you want to see me? I hope you had no intention of asking me to be a back-up speaker in case he turned you down?' James laughed.

'Not quite' he said, 'although I do feel that Donald should at least discuss what he intends to say with you before he stands up.'

'What do you need me for then?' Colin asked.

'Well, there are to be some informal discussions in groups about this and other subjects as part of the Conference this year. The whole meeting seems to grow bigger each year. One of the other groups is going to discuss how to integrate young people into the Church better, especially in this computer driven world we now find ourselves in. It is becoming an ever increasingly materialistic world and we all felt that someone with your background – teaching and dealing with youngsters – might give the group a valuable insight that could inform their discussions. We hope that you might feel you could help?'

Colin didn't hesitate.

'Of course if you feel I can add anything to discussions like that, I would be only too glad to help'.

'Good' James said. 'I wanted to get an answer on that from you before I explained that apparently, one of the hierarchy of the Church of England is going to be a part of that discussion group. There are some efforts being made to get a closer relationship between the two churches and he has specifically asked to come and be a part of the group looking at young people as he is particularly interested in their futures within the Church.'

'Do we know who it is going to be yet?' Colin queried.

James looked at his notes. 'It says here on this proposed programme of events that it is the Bishop of Winchester. His name is The Right Reverend Walter Walken. Under English Law, he is one of the five Bishops who sit as the Lords Spiritual in the House of Lords.

'I had to look this up, because it is so very different to our own way of doing things. Apparently there are five so-called 'great sees' in the Church of England, because they were among the first to be created as the church expanded in the early days. The holder of this title sits in the Lords because of this fact rather than because of his own seniority within the Church hierarchy. This Walter Walken was selected by the present Prime Minister just two years ago. These changes do not happen very often as you might imagine, and the Prime Minister attended his investiture in Winchester shortly afterwards.

'It looks like you will be meeting a real V.I.P. when you sit down to discuss the agenda with him, Colin.' Donald said. 'You are now moving in very high circles. I wonder if you'll be expected to stand whenever he comes into the room.'

Colin smiled and said 'You've always been the one to puncture pomposity, but I can do it too, you know. In any case, he might not be like that at all. I will wait until I can make judgments for myself – as always.'

'It seems that there is only one further question that needs to be asked then, eh?' Donald said.

'What's that?' James replied.

'Where is this magnificent array of talent to be convening

this year? Donald asked. 'I hope it's not too far away. Mum will need to be left on her own while we are both away, and I wouldn't want that to be for too long. Neighbours are fine, but they are not family.'

'Actually, the conference this year is returning to somewhere it last met nearly twenty years ago. Pontypridd in South Wales will be hosting it, with some of the accommodations held in the town itself and others down the road in Cardiff. As luck would have it, you couldn't really get much closer, could you? No trips to Bora Bora or anything like that for you.'

As the two brothers walked back up the slope to see their mother later, Colin said 'we should maybe get in touch with Rhona. She is too far away most of the time for us to be able to meet up, but I seem to remember she now has a boyfriend who hails from somewhere in South Wales. Perhaps she can get over there to coincide with our visit. It would be nice to play catch up a little, don't you think?'

'I suppose so' Donald replied 'but if she is cohabiting out of wedlock, as seems to be the norm these days, I won't promise to keep quiet about it.'

'I should imagine she will be more than a match for you, if you start that kind of conversation, and if she isn't, I am. Remember I said that.'

* * * *

When Peter and Rhona arrived at Gareth's house after the drive up from London earlier that day, Samantha was just about to go to bed. As the little girl came over and gave them both a goodnight hug, she said

'will I see you tomorrow when I wake up?'

'Of course you will, darling' Rhona said.

'And can we go somewhere nice then?'

'Your Mummy and I will take you somewhere nice, that's a promise, OK'

Samantha nodded vigorously. She turned as she was about to go up the stairs with Maddie and said, 'I like you, I think you're pretty.'

As Maddie smiled and took the little girl upstairs, Peter could see the look in Rhona's eyes. Maybe, he thought, it was about time they started to have 'that talk'.

Nathan and Daniel were already upstairs playing on their latest tablets before going to sleep themselves. When Rhona had raised an enquiring eyebrow at that, Maddie had explained that it was one of the 'treats' they had developed recently. It was only at weekends that they were allowed an extra half hour like that, as there was no homework to be done for the next day.

After they had eaten, the four adults settled themselves comfortably and Gareth said, 'now little brother, what brings you down into deepest Wales then?'

'Does there have to be a reason?'

'I think so. You are both – he nodded to Rhona – so busy in your own lives, that I know it is difficult to find time for anything else. The fact that you're here, tells me that there is something special happening in your neck of the woods that has become important enough to make the effort.'

'Are you perhaps thinking of tying the knot?' Maddie said.

Peter and Rhona both smiled. Peter said, 'that is something we are only starting to discuss, but it isn't what brought us down here. I would like to hear your views on what is happening right now at our research facility. Everyone down there is forever talking about what is going on in the South East of England as if that is the only part of the country which matters. I felt the need for a dose of South Wales realism.'

'Tell me more' Gareth said.

23.

IT HAD BEEN a rough passage through the Bay of Biscay. None of the group were sailors, and some had spent a lot of time on deck giving their latest meals back to the ocean. Yousuf had been one of those, but was not as bad as the others. He had eaten as little as possible because he needed to keep his wits about him and be aware of what was going on around him. He needed to be alert to any information that he might need to pass on to Omar. All he knew to date was that they were travelling on the M.V. Marianas. That might become useful, and he would break his silence soon even if that was all he was going to able to pass on. When Ahmed called them all together he hoped that they were going to be told more.

They could see from the deck a large lighthouse and some low laying land behind it. One of the others asked where they were. The man who they had come to recognise as the one who was in charge of the organisation of the trip, Adisa Folami, was passing the group and heard the question.

'That lighthouse is on the North Western tip of France and the land further away is the Isle of Ushant' he said. 'We will be turning east shortly to begin our run along the North Western coastline of France. In another thirty miles or so we will be passing the tallest lighthouse in the whole of France, le Phare de l'ile Vierge. Just after that we will be taking on board two more passengers. They will be acting as guides for us. They have a local knowledge of the English Channel better than we do, and they will make sure we reach the coastline without falling foul of any dangerous or hidden rocks etc. We should be off the coast of England soon, maybe early tomorrow, if the wind keeps from the same direction and the seas stay as they are.' He nodded to Ahmed as he turned and walked away.

After Adisa had moved on, Ahmed started to speak.

'I know you will all be keen to find out a little more of what we intend to do. I have been waiting until now to say something because it is always unwise to go into detail until it is absolutely necessary.' They all nodded.

'When we arrive in England, we will split up immediately. Four of us will go with the friends who will be meeting us and travel into London itself. There you will be ready for action – against the very heart of their Government. That will happen after the other two begin their own action. That will be against one of the senior figures in the government.

I had intended that Rifat would join me in that work, but he is no longer with us. I have decided that you', he turned to Yousuf, 'will join me instead. Your expertise with small arms might become very useful.' Yousuf could not contain his glee. He let it show, knowing that the others would put a different interpretation on his reactions.

'Our friends who are already in place in England' Ahmed

went on 'will be ready to mount an attack on the Prime Minister's official residence in Downing Street. It is well guarded as you might expect, but it is in the centre of the city and, as such, is open to a number of ways of mounting an attack. Our friends have been watching the area for some long time, and have identified times when there is a good possibility of dealing a blow that will reverberate around the world. If we are able to identify in advance when Ministers are coming there for a meeting, we can be certain that we will have an opportunity to dispatch at least some of them to their maker. It may be, of course' he went on 'that some of you will die in the process. There are plans for escape afterwards, but we cannot be certain how things will develop after the shooting starts. Be assured that if any of you do find yourselves talking to Allah himself, he will have a smile on his face when he greets you.'

Yousuf felt on safe enough ground to ask,

'Where are we going to land then, Ahmed? The south of England is highly populated and we presumably need to arrive unseen.'

'That is what I think those who might want to stop us would expect.' Ahmed replied. 'And that is why we will be landing in their midst. There are several parts of those southern shores which are difficult and even dangerous to try and come ashore near. The very fact that it is a busy coastline will mean that a small boat carrying half a dozen men coming in to land will not cause too much discussion if anyone sees us, provided we do it openly.'

'All I can say at the moment is we will not be very far from our separate targets when we do land. Exactly where, we will decide when I speak (he held up his own mobile phone) to our friends later. Tides and the weather may change things a little, but rest assured we have friends waiting for us. They, and the two others that Adisa referred to, will make sure we come ashore safely, and then take us on our way, as quickly as possible.'

That final statement from Ahmed told Yousuf that he was not going to be able to give more details to Omar. It was, he reckoned, always going to be difficult to make a worthwhile contact from the boat. Talking carried a significant risk of being overheard, and even texting might be interrupted. If either of those things were to happen, he knew he would not be able to dispose of any resultant body as easily as he had with Rifat.

* * * *

The phone dealer had been as good as his word. Although it was now several days since Yousuf had bought the phone, the battery was only now beginning to show signs of needing charging. He hoped there would be enough left to allow Omar to keep a tag on exactly where they were, but he still didn't know with any certainty where, or when, they were going to touch land. He couldn't ask again either. One too many questions would almost certainly make Ahmed wonder why. No, he would just have to be patient and hope that he could still get something out in time to prevent whatever was being planned taking place.

Ahmed had already mentioned Downing Street, but Yousuf reasoned that a target like this would already be well recognised by the anti-terrorist units in the Country. The other target was much more specific. A leading member of the Government, yet still vague enough to make Yousuf wait until it became clearer. There was always a slim possibility that he might get the chance to send out one message – there was no chance he would get two out. At least he was going to be part of that action and might be able to have an effect on the eventual outcome – as long as Ahmed had no doubts about him.

24.

PETER THOMAS WAS glad he had made the effort to come and see Gareth. He wished he could say the same about his old man. Gareth had, of course told Bryn that his younger son was coming over for the weekend, and that he was invited for a meal together with the two boys and their wives/partners on the Saturday evening.

It had not gone well but then, Peter reflected, it never did. There was a strained atmosphere almost from the moment he stepped inside the front door. After shaking hands, he went on to give the grandchildren some sweets he had brought. Maddie had said that they should wait until after they'd had their evening meal before they could eat them. That clearly didn't please Bryn.

'I thought they could have at least a couple now as they know they are here for them.'

Maddie, however, had stood her ground.

'They are a treat, not a substitute for real food. They can have some later.' Peter knew he should have kept out of it, after all they weren't his kids were they? But he didn't.

'You were never happy when we wanted sweets at whatever you considered to be the wrong time, were you? Now you should be able to let Gareth and Maddie bring up their kids in their own way. You were always telling our Nannie and Grandad exactly that weren't you?'

There was, of course, no answer to that. Bryn stamped away and sat down. It didn't get any better. After they had all sat down for a meal, with the kids safely upstairs, Bryn asked Peter what had led to the 'honour' of this visit. Rhona flashed warning signals to Peter about his response, but he was ready.

'I wanted some sound advice about some important things that are happening down south, and I knew that my big brother was someone I could trust to give it to me fairly. I don't have many people I can trust like that.'

'You could have asked me' Bryn said.

'You don't really need me to answer that do you Father?' Peter said a little more loudly than was really necessary.

Bryn looked as if he was about to come back at him, but Gareth interrupted before another argument could develop further.

'Peter has been telling us that Mum was asking when we might be able to take the kids down to see her. Maddie and I are thinking we might manage to do that during the next half-term break. She doesn't see the grandchildren as often as she would like, I know, so that might be nice. While we are always busy at the garage, I thought, if you had enough notice, you would be able to hold the fort for a few days when we went. You could manage that, couldn't you?'

'I suppose so' Bryn replied and everyone else heaved a sigh of relief that the moment had passed.

In an effort to move the conversation away from the dangerous waters it seemed to be heading towards, Maddie said she was annoyed about the discussions she had had with Sandra Wilson, the Headmistress at Nathan's Primary school. Bryn asked what had happened, and listened closely as she recounted the meeting she had had with Mrs Wilson. Rhona was first to respond.

'I think that's dreadful that a mark should be put against Nathan's record over something as trivial as that.' Before anyone else could say anything, Bryn jumped in.

'I'm now Chairman of the Education Committee in Newport and I can confirm that the whole South Wales Area is under close scrutiny. There are people in London who are saying that something needs to be done about the level of achievement recorded in this area, it simply isn't good enough.'

There were several other 'moments' throughout the meal, notably when Bryn tried to find out exactly what his ex-wife was now doing. Peter had no intention of giving him too much ammunition which both boys knew he would then try and use against their mother. Even after all this time, the old man still felt the need to control everyone in his life, or anyone – like Sally – who ever had been in his life. Words like 'seems to be doing fine' and 'I've been very busy on some bits of my research lately and so I haven't been in touch with her for a little while' were true, but didn't really answer the old man's questions.

It was a relief to both Gareth and Peter when the old man

Beyond Tomorrow

eventually got up to say goodbye. Bryn's farewell request to Peter to 'keep in touch' as they stood at the door was agreed to with some alacrity, and promptly forgotten the moment the door closed.

* * * *

Samantha cuddled Rhona and was reluctant to let her go the next afternoon as she and Peter got in their car for the drive south. Eventually she brightened when Rhona and Maddie agreed that they would come to see her again 'soon'. Peter and Gareth hugged with a feeling that belied their understanding that distances would always mean that the two brothers would see each other less frequently than either wanted.

As they drove away on the Sunday afternoon and started to get back into 'South of England' mould, Rhona looked across at Peter and said

'Was the journey worth while, then?'

'Yes, of course' he replied.

'Even the visit from your father?' she queried.

'Especially the visit from him. It proved – if I ever needed the proof – that he has not changed, and never will. That is sad, but as he never tired of telling us when we were growing up 'who said life had to be fair'. That always came out while he was refusing to do something that one of us wanted – even my mother. It became something of a mantra in the house for occasions when he would just walk away rather than help.'

'And Gareth?' she prompted.

'Gareth gave me the advice I needed, as I knew he would. I suppose, I already knew what I needed to do, but it was good to hear him say it out loud. I felt like walking away from the Research Institute before I came here. It is looking so much like my work is going to be twisted and corrupted for shallow political ends that I had seriously been thinking about a move abroad.'

'There are at least two Universities in the US that have already asked me to think about joining them. Almost unlimited funds and a refreshing desire to let me get on with it, rather than interfere at every turn, is quite enticing. In the end, though, as Gareth said, I would always be unhappy at the thought of someone else taking over here and perhaps taking it all in a very different direction.'

'The real killer in his arguments was that, if I stayed here, I might still be able to influence for the better what they are trying to do. He said that was a decision that only I could take, but he suggested that it might be worthwhile to think whether my research was important enough to me to get involved in what would likely be lots of arguments, some of which I would probably not win.'

'He refused to say what he thought I should do about that, but we know each other well enough that I did not have to hear him say what I knew would be his view. In the end, I realised that the research I'm involved in is something that I think is worth fighting for.'

'Then that's it settled, isn't it?' Rhona said. 'We're going to put up a fight – together.' He smiled and slid his hand into hers for a moment.

'We're going to do a lot more together, aren't we?'

'I don't think Samantha would forgive us if we didn't. She has already asked if she can be a bridesmaid.'

'And what did you say?'

'There is only one answer a little girl like that wants to hear, and I couldn't possibly have disappointed her, could I?'

* * * *

As the M.V. Marianas sailed past the red and white lighthouse, Yousuf knew where they were. He had been an avid student of Geology at school, giving him, as it did, an entirely different view of his world. He even remembered with some pleasure the film that had fired his interest. Jurassic Park had shown him a history like nothing he had ever imagined. He had read several geological books at the time, and one had gone into some great detail in describing the different geological Eras. One of these, the Mesolithic Era, had been illustrated with examples of places showing where this era could still be seen on the surface of the planet. The Portland Bill lighthouse had been one of those illustrations and he had no difficulty in recognising it now.

He did not have much time to take in the view however, as Ahmed appeared on deck shortly after they had left the lighthouse behind and said it was time to get changed into the clothes they had brought with them. Twenty minutes later they were all on deck again dressed as casual travellers. All of them would have passed for Spaniards or even Greeks, and they all looked at each other and smiled.

He realised that he was not going to have any opportunity to text, far less make a voice call before they disembarked. That was just going to be too bad. Omar might still be able to keep tabs on his whereabouts using the transponder built into the mobile phone he had bought, but perhaps not closely enough to have any affect on whatever Ahmed was planning. He would be on his own on that. Yousuf had no problems with that situation. The last few years had shown that he was capable of handling most things he came up against. Even if he could not do that, he would at least come face to face with Allah secure in the knowledge that he had tried.

* * * *

As Adam Clayton pulled his car up outside the boathouse at the edge of Kimmeridge Bay, he sat back and smiled. Life was good, he felt. He had a wife who had given him two of the most pleasant natured boys one could wish for, and a job working as an Engineer – now Chief Engineer, he reminded himself – with Cross Channel Ferries in Poole along the coast. Now he had a little boat he could make seaworthy and spend time sailing around Weymouth Bay with his boys. He had almost missed the chance to buy the boat. Luckily one of his friends at work had noticed the 'for sale' notice in the local paper. With his recent promotion, he had managed to scrape together enough funds to buy it. It needed work doing on it to make it truly seaworthy, but he would enjoy that too. It would make him feel even more that it was his boat rather than just something he had bought because he had the money.

There were not many boats around today. Of course it was mid-week, so all the weekenders would not be there. His shift working patterns reflected the sailing schedules of the ferries rather than anything else, so he often had time to spare in the middle of the week like this. It meant that the boys could not come with him of course. Schooling was more important, but he had promised them he would bring them out at the weekend, if he could just get some of the work done today.

There were nearly always boats out in the bay however, so when he heard the scrape as a boat came up one of the slipways as he ferreted around inside the boathouse for the tools he knew he would need, he paid no attention. It was only when he emerged from the darkness that he saw the group of men who had clearly arrived in the small boat he had heard earlier. A car and a van were coming down the gravel path from what passed as a main road in this area. He wondered if it was some of the other owners whom he might soon be able to call friends.

As he started to walk towards the car, he was only vaguely aware that the men who had landed at the slipway were also coming up behind him. He turned towards them just in time to see the flashing knife that the man in the lead held in his hand. He was not in time to stop it entering his rib cage. As he was falling to the ground with blood already coming out between his shirt buttons, he realised too late that he would never be able to make friends with the men in the car, or anyone else, ever again.

Yousuf was aghast. Although he realised that the group didn't want to be seen landing like this, he had not anticipated the speed which Ahmed had shown as he raced in front of them up to the man who had just come out of the boathouse. Before Yousuf could do or say anything, it was already too late. As the man collapsed in a heap on the ground, Ahmed was ordering two of the others to put the body at the back of the boathouse. 'With luck' he said 'we will be well on our way before he is discovered'.

As Yousuf got in the back of the car, and Ahmed slid into the front passenger seat, he made a note that he would be ready for the next time. Ahmed had clearly wanted to show everyone else in the rest of his little group that he was a man of action. Yousuf would demonstrate when the time came, that he was a man of action too, and the next time he would be far quicker than he had been today.

25.

COLIN AND DONALD MCLEOD took their church responsibilities very seriously. They knew that while Donald was to be delivering a keynote speech to the whole assembly, Colin's involvement was likely to be just as crucial to the future direction of their beloved Free Church. As a result they agreed to sit down several days later and show each other what they were preparing in advance of making the trip to South Wales.

They hadn't got very far when Colin's mobile rang. Picking it up, he heard the voice of their niece Rhona.

'Hi Uncle Colin' she said. 'I'm making arrangements to come over to Newport sometime soon. Peter and I are spending some time with Gareth, Peter's older brother and his family. Mum told me you and Donald were coming down this way for some kind of Conference soon, and I just wondered if you can fit some time in to your busy schedule so that we could have a little reunion. It would be really nice to meet up. It's been such a long time.'

'That would be nice' Colin replied. 'I had already suggested to Donald that we should make contact, but as always, other things intruded. We will have some free time on the Sunday. You know that our church rather frowns on work being done during the Sabbath. Most of the other delegates are using it either to attend a church service, or visit one of the tourist attractions down here. If you would like, I will talk to Donald and get him to come with me.'

'That would be brilliant' she replied. 'Peter would like the chance to make contact with you, as I've told him all about the family.'

'Consider it a date then' Colin said.

They exchanged details of the dates that fitted with the brothers' travel, and Rhona said 'leave it with me, will you? I'll speak to Maddie, Gareth's wife. She will know where we could go that will do an old fashioned Sunday lunch. That would seem to fit the bill, eh?'

'Sounds good to me.'

* * * *

Peter Thomas knew he should have been pleased. He also knew that he wasn't. The amount of 'extra' money being made available for his research was something that many of his colleagues would have died for. The fact that much of the money had been taken from their budgets at very short notice, had not made him the flavour of the month when he had taken his normal seat in the staff canteen in recent days. Many of the other research leaders were angry and envious at one and the same time.

Now that he was going in to see Arnold, he hoped he

would find out what lay behind this change of emphasis towards his work. He also hoped some of his wilder fears as to what it might all mean would prove to be groundless, but a small insistent voice inside his head said otherwise.

26.

PETER THOMAS AND Geoffrey Williams were both lost in their own thoughts as they approached the small conference room. They had spent some time together since the new emphasis had been placed on Peter's development work. The old phrase 'two heads are better than one' had proven to be accurate on this occasion more than once. They were pretty sure that they had nearly all the 'hardware' issues resolved. The miniaturisation of the receptors had been concluded successfully. They could now be inserted through a large, but still fairly ordinary needle such as those used for the delivery of medical vaccines.

The development of a fully organic receptor/transmitter had been the most difficult aspect to their joint work. That had enabled a smaller needle to be used for the insertion part of the process, while allowing for a more natural movement within the subject after insertion. The earlier attempts using a part organic/part electronic receptor had suffered due to the body's natural response to foreign bodies being used. They were aware of the likelihood of a rejection – it was no more than the first of the replacement lung or kidney pioneers had come across all those years ago. It had still held them up – but not any more.

There was however some difficulties in terms of the insertion process. When Geoffrey had looked at the system for the army in the field, he had initially worked on the premise that a 'shot' in the upper arm would suffice to insert a receptor. That had been changed after discussion to an injection at the base of the neck. Now that they were talking about a more sophisticated system which would directly affect the neuron pathways in the brain, a different approach had shown itself to be necessary.

While the neuron receptors were organic based to enable them to 'grow' and become an integral part of the brain, the use of organic material in this way meant that they had to be in place fairly quickly. Insertion of a foreign body into the body activated a natural response from the immune system. If the time lapse between insertion and proper placement in the body was too long, the Immune System could and would attempt to destroy the invader.

Geoffrey had initially suggested that they employ the same procedure of an injection at the top of the spine as he had already used for the military. However, when they got down to it, they both agreed that if there was likely to be arguments against such an injection, it was more than likely to come from special interest groups on the basis of 'civil liberties'. They decided that it was better to revert to the shot in the arm that he had started with. That decision, in turn, had led to changes in the molecular composition of the receptor to help it to move through the upper body more quickly. Geoffrey had described it as like using a slide rather than a stepladder to get from A to B, and Peter did not disagree with that somewhat simple assessment. Tests on laboratory animals had now shown that this movement could be speeded up to the point where there were only a small number of receptors which did not make the journey successfully.

One of the successes of their joint efforts had been that the Transmission of data (or instructions as Peter continually reminded himself) could now 'piggy-back' on Geoffrey's SPPS technology. This had as its most important feature, the ability for this data to be transmitted over a far greater distance than before.

The part of the work which still gave cause for concern was (as it had been from the beginning) the range of responses which might be generated in any subject. There were so many variables at play in that area, that neither man was content that it was ready for use outside of the laboratory environment, and was unlikely to become so in the foreseeable future.

As Peter turned the doorknob and they went into the room, they were amazed to see more people there than they had anticipated. Arnold Patterson was there, of course, and they weren't all that surprised to see Eric Mercer also there. He had been around the place quite a lot recently, so finding him in the chair was only to be expected. There were, however another three people there, none of them known to either Peter or Geoffrey.

Alexander Cowan (call me Alex), it turned out, was a

deputy Minister in the Home Office reporting to Hilary Watson specifically on Immigration issues. Graham Mountjoy was an Under Secretary at the Ministry of Defence and he had brought Commander Ramsey along with him. The Commander, it turned out, was the Senior Medical Officer in the Military (Naval Branch). Peter and Geoffrey raised their eyebrows but said nothing.

It was Eric Mercer who spoke first. 'Tell me – us – Peter where you are at with your research, will you? I think I'm fairly well up to speed on the latest position, but our friends here may well appreciate finding out how things stand right now.'

'Well Minister' Peter said 'we think we've cracked most of the hardware issues, but we are still needing some considerable work to be done before the software programming is complete, and in any case we are a long way from saying that it is a project which is ready to leave the laboratory environment.'

'How do you propose that the – receptors I think you call them? – are put in place?' Commander Ramsey asked. Before either Geoffrey or Peter could reply, Alexander Cowan interjected.

'I don't wish to stifle discussion here gentlemen, but I could just get a feel for the big picture and then leave you all to chat about the minutiae? My lady boss has a meeting scheduled with the PM later today and she needs to be up to speed by the time she talks to him.' Eric Mercer looked slightly put out, but merely said 'and what would you like to know that will be enough for her ladyship to be 'up to speed'?

'I think the lady will want to know that the hardware, as you call it, is both working and available. If it is not available right now, she will want to know what kind of timescale you assess will be required before it is ready for use.

Eric Mercer looked at Peter and Geoffrey. Geoffrey took the lead. 'I think the hardware issues are all now resolved. I have been more on the supply side of the effort than the programming, but there we are still generating orders for needles and ancillary equipment. The receptors have all been fully designed – he looked in Peter's direction and got an affirmative nod – and we are discussing who among the pharmaceutical companies we normally use are best placed to produce the numbers we envisage. We also need to be certain that all the quality control issues have been thoroughly worked out and that there will be no nasty surprises in that respect. I would guess' he said looking at Alex 'that we will have several batches available in the next month or so, say fifty to a hundred units.' He couldn't resist finishing with the barb 'if we had not been asked to come here like this, the orders might well have gone out today.'

Peter realised that he was fighting something of a losing battle, but he had to say his piece. 'Remember, we have *NOT* fully tested the software on this. We have no way we can be certain about the effect on any subject we try to send instructions to after it is injected into their system.' Eric Mercer was more than aware that everything said in this room would be relayed to both the Home Secretary as well as the Prime Minister. When it came right down to it, he would rather upset one of his own scientists than either of his ministerial seniors.

'Your reservations are duly noted' he said.

The meeting broke up shortly afterwards, leaving Peter spitting blood.

27.

HILARY WATSON PULLED into her drive in the village of Four Marks and switched the Mercedes engine off. It had been another long day after another long week, and she was looking forward to a night of freedom from the interminable wrangles she had been dealing with all week. Sally had agreed to make her dinner tonight before she left for her own house. That would be good Hilary thought. She still had a couple of bottles of that lovely Burgundy that Laithwaites had delivered a few weeks ago in the kitchen to make sure they were at room temperature. She would open one tonight. She deserved it after the week she had put in.

She sat down a little later on the settee in her lounge, after what had been a beautiful rib-eye steak. She was already on her third glass, but she knew there was nothing wrong with her eyesight as she bent over to switch the TV on and catch the late evening news. She had caught a movement outside through the large French windows of her Conservatory. She looked up sharply, but there was nothing to be seen. She briefly wondered if she should activate the panic button that all senior Cabinet Ministers now had nearby as a matter of course. She went to the window and looked out, just in time to see the cat from next door activate the second security light in the back garden. Fool, she thought to herself. Can you imagine what the papers would make of it if they knew that the Home Secretary had called out the security detail for a cat! She sat back down after filling her glass again.

As the news went on she slowly lost interest. She had come to realise that most news items, especially those related to the comings and goings at Westminster, were notoriously inaccurate. Newscasters these days seemed to see themselves as making the news more than just reporting it. She remembered with disgust the newscasters in Portugal all those years ago – interviewing each other for God's sake! – when that little girl had gone missing while on holiday. All because they had no real information to tell viewers. They didn't care if they were causing even more stress to the parents, as long as they got a story out to meet their schedules. What had been her name? Oh yes, Madeleine McCann. They never had found the little girl and she felt sad for a moment at the torment that those parents must have been suffering at the time – and forever more she didn't doubt.

As she was going upstairs to bed fifteen minutes later having made sure the house was secure and the lights were out, the security light at the back came on again. She ignored it this time.

She got undressed and then put on the silk pyjamas that her father had given her for last Christmas. It was as close as he had ever come to thinking about her as anything more than just another woman, but she liked the feel of them against her skin. As she went into the en-suite to comb her hair, she heard the crash as someone broke through the glass panel on the kitchen door downstairs. Instinctively, she pressed the panic button under the carpet in front of the toilet in her en-suite – the one she had objected to having fitted – and then turned to run for the phone on her bedside table, as she heard the heavy footsteps of someone running upstairs. She cursed silently to herself that the phone was at the other side of the king size bed she had bought only recently. She never shut her bedroom door. Why would she, when she was alone in the house? This allowed the heavily bearded man to come in and launch himself across the bed as she tried to get to the phone – in vain. Their hands closed on the phone at the same time. He tore it from her grasp before she could activate it, and then rolled over and knocked her to the floor.

As she staggered to her feet, she heard someone else coming up the stairs. She realised there was nowhere for her to run to, and so she got up and stood silently at the foot of the bed until she was prodded into movement by the first man using the gun he was carrying. He signalled to her to go back downstairs and she followed him while the other one came down behind her. The man in the lead shoved her roughly towards the settee she had vacated only a few minutes ago. 'Sit' he commanded.

The intruders clearly didn't know about the panic button she had already activated. There was a fail-safe system in place, as had been explained when the Security Service had installed their hardware. If she pressed a button by mistake – when he saw the look on her face as he described the

Beyond Tomorrow

procedure, he had assured her that it did indeed happen –
then she had to ring the number he provided within two
minutes of the error. They would then know not to send out
the cavalry. She hadn't made that phone call of course, and
so now the duty control officer would have been alerted and
would regard it as an intrusion. Others would then come
running. She hoped they would get here soon enough. She
did not want to become the main player in a possible hostage
scenario.

'Who are you, what do you want?' she asked.

He spun round and slapped her hard across the mouth
with his gun hand, drawing blood as he did so. 'Shut up' he
snarled at her as the second man came into the room and,
going swiftly to the curtains both front and back, drew them
closed.

Ahmed, the one who had run up stairs and prevented
her from using the phone, turned to Yousuf and said 'fetch
something to tie her with'. Yousuf went. When he returned
Ahmed was still standing with the gun in his hand that he
was brandishing in the direction of Hilary. As Yousuf moved
towards Hilary he said 'What do you intend to do with her
now Ahmed?'

Ahmed snarled back at him 'no names!'

Yousuf replied 'does it matter? You wanted to let the
whole world know who we are and what we are doing. Why
should knowledge of our names be so secret?'

'Just tie her up for now, I have to make a phone call. Then
we will see.' With that he disappeared into the kitchen.

When Ahmed reappeared a few minutes later, Hilary was securely gagged and tied to the wooden chair she normally used for working on her laptop. Yousuf looked questioningly at Ahmed. Ahmed slipped into Arabic and said 'alttakhallus min laha alan' – dispose of her now. 'We will then leave to rejoin our comrades in London. If we leave her here as an obvious sacrifice, the British Government will expend energy – useless energy and resources – trying to find out who did this. That should make it a little easier to carry out the rest of the plan. The Security Services will be stretched to near breaking point when they have to deal with something like this against one of their senior politicians. When the second part of the plan is put into effect, it will send a clear message to these infidels, and to the rest of the world.' With that, he turned and approached the bound woman, levelling his gun at her as he did so. Hilary's eyes widened as she saw what was about to happen.

Yousuf didn't have time to protest, or ask any other questions which might have delayed matters. Immediate action was the only solution to the situation. Even as he sprang forward, the use of the word sacrifice made his mind flit back to that day all those years ago when he had stood in the heat looking at four newly dug graves. He did not need reminding who it was who had caused him so much grief. Ahmed must have seen him coming out of the corner of his eye, but assumed that he was about to join in. He was right about that, but not in the way that Ahmed thought. Yousuf's knife entered Ahmed's torso slightly left of his backbone and was driven up into the heart with immense force as Yousuf exacted the revenge that he had waited for, for so long.

Ahmed half turned in surprise, his brain not yet registering the pain which came a moment later. As he collapsed to the floor dropping his gun into the pool of blood which was rapidly spreading across the pale beige carpet, his eyes looked puzzled. As Hilary's eyes widened even further, Yousuf knelt beside the body of the dying man and said 'you made sacrifices of my parents, my wife, my little boy – my whole family – in a Mosque a long time ago, and now I am making one of you.' Then he ever so deliberately spat into the man's face. That action was the last thing that Ahmed Chisisi saw and felt in this world.

As Yousuf stood and walked over to where Hilary Watson was tied to the chair, she started to struggle against her ropes. He realised she thought he might be going to do the same to her as she had just seen him do to Ahmed. It was only as he raised his fingers to his lips that he became aware that he still held the blood-stained knife in his hands. He smiled and laid the knife on the coffee table, then approached her. He released the gag and asked her not to scream while he untied the ropes.

He hadn't finished untying her, when there was a crash as the front door was kicked in and a number of heavily armed men, faces covered in Balaclava's and wearing riot protection gear, swarmed into the lounge. Two immediately ran upstairs while another two came in – literally – through the rear kitchen door. The first man inside the lounge had already slammed Yousuf onto the ground and knelt on his back.

Hilary was quick to regain her composure. 'It's OK officer. I think he's on our side' she said. The Elite Squad Officer said 'we'll make those judgements later Mam. For now, just stay still and stay quiet.' She was about to reply along the lines of 'who do you think you are ordering me around?', but she decided that, for once in her life, she should do as she was told.

Less than twenty minutes later, Hilary was in the back of a car on her way with three of the men to the Military Hospital in Bordon, while Yousuf was propelled into the back of a van with more of the men seated either side of him on his way to the secure section of the Military base at the same place.

28.

As Rhona McLeod ordered a 'special breakfast' at Benito's, the cafe – cum – Italian Restaurant in Risca's High Street, she knew she was a little early for her get together with Madeleine Thomas. She was looking forward to seeing Madeleine and her little girl Samantha again. Samantha had, apparently never stopped talking about becoming a bridesmaid after she and Peter had visited Madeleine and Gareth. Madeleine had suggested that, when she had time, it would be lovely to see each other again, and Rhona felt it would be good too. She was so far away from her own home in Stornoway, and all her erstwhile school chums, that it would be nice to find someone she could talk to, just like she used to confide in her mother back home. Madeleine had shown that she was the kind of woman she felt she could confide in if she ever had problems, and she didn't want to see that possibility disappear just because they had to make an effort to see each other.

Peter hadn't made the trip over to Wales this time. He was completely snowed under at work trying to develop the software to the point where it could be used 'in the field' as he described it. She was almost as unhappy at its intended use as he was, but she knew she would get nowhere in protesting on her own. Anyway, as Peter had said, there is a long way between developing software and making it work correctly in all circumstances. He felt sure that problems would arise quite naturally as situations they had not planned for showed themselves. She wasn't so sure difficulties of that kind would stop what she now saw as a political juggernaut gaining momentum, but she had kept quiet.

She was reading the Guardian to get their 'take' on the consequences of the attack on Hilary Watson. It had been all over the TV news channels until she was ready to scream at them. She knew they had to fill air time, but really! There must have been other newsworthy items they could have been reporting on, but no, in today's world it was much easier to endlessly repeat the same old statements – every five minutes! – until she could almost recite it word for word. At least the broadsheets tried to give a little more depth of thought to what they wrote. As a result, she barely noticed the couple who came into the cafe and sat down a couple of tables away.

It was only when the waitress brought the food out for her that she looked up. She could hardly believe her eyes. Just then the man looked over in her direction and she could see the puzzlement in his eyes which quickly changed to a big smile on his face. 'Rhona, Rhona McLeod, is it really you?' he said. She smiled in return and said 'I'm afraid it is Gordon.' They both stood up and he came over and gave her a big hug.

'Where did you pop up from?' he enquired.

'I could ask the same question of you' she responded.

'I thought you were down somewhere in the South of England.'

'Yes I am normally, but my partner's family hail from nearby and I've come up to spend a little time with a little girl who might become my niece shortly.'

He broke off at the words partner, and turned to his companion. 'Rachel, meet Rhona McLeod from Stornoway.'

After the formal introductions had been done, Gordon Morrison suggested that they could all sit together; otherwise Rhona's meal would quickly get cold. It didn't take him long to bring Rhona up to speed on what he had been doing since they last saw each other and she did likewise. She was just finishing her meal when a squeal from the doorway announced the arrival of Madeleine and Samantha.

Gordon rose to make way for the newcomers.

'It's OK Gordon' Rhona said. 'I've promised this little girl a treat and I wouldn't like to disappoint her,' as she took Samantha's hand. 'Perhaps we might meet again, though, after all I'll be coming up here a bit more often now that I've got someone like this to see.' She squeezed Samantha's hand again and was rewarded by a beam that stretched from ear to ear.

'Let me know when you're coming back then' Gordon replied. 'Rachel likes to get down here to see her parents from time to time, and we might well be able to coordinate our visits.'

'That would be good' Rhona said 'Perhaps we could all

go out for a meal the next time. I'm sure Gareth and Maddie would love to do that, wouldn't you?' she said to Madeleine.' A simple nod answered that.

'That's a date then' Gordon said.

As she left, she exchanged business cards with Gordon, saying 'we must try and keep in touch more often now that we've made contact again'. He agreed and said 'I haven't forgotten the help you gave me when I arrived in Stornoway. If there is ever anything I can do to help pay that debt back, you have only to ask. Remember that.'

* * * *

It had turned out to be a fairly tortuous route flying from Stornoway to Cardiff. The interim stop at Glasgow where they had to disembark before changing aircraft had merely elongated what was already a difficult journey. 'No Jumbo jets here' Donald McLeod had said as they settled back into their seats on the elderly Loganair 50 seater Saab 2000 for the take off on the outskirts of their home town. Hanging about in Glasgow airport for the connection to Cardiff was a real pain. Donald said 'I wonder if they deliberately do it like this to encourage everyone to spend more money in the airport shops?'

At least the second leg of the journey was a little more comfortable as the Flybe (previously Jersey European Airways) Embraer E-195 took off. It had a capacity of 118 and there were no more than 75 passengers, mainly business men, on board. Luckily they had a member of the organising committee on hand as they disembarked in Cardiff in order to collect them and take them to their hotel on the outskirts of Pontypridd itself.

The Heritage Park Hotel was small but well furnished and Colin and Donald had been booked into one of the few twin rooms available. The feature they liked best was the fact that it had once been a church, albeit not a Free Church building. After they had settled in and had a relaxing meal in the olde worlde dining room, complete with a stained glass window which reinforced the origins of the establishment, they started to look over their notes again. They were deep into that discussion when Colin's phone bleeped. When he answered it was Rhona.

'Hi Uncle Colin. I've arranged for us all to meet up at a place out in the country a bit called the Maenllwyd Inn. It's the other side of Caerphilly for you. I've even managed to arrange for one of our old friends to be there too. Gordon Morrison, you remember him?, is coming down from North Wales at the same time.'

'He's in North Wales?'

'Yes. He and his girlfriend Rachel – I've met her, she's a lovely girl – now live in Barmouth, but Rachel originally hails from just outside Newport. I met them, quite by chance, the last time I was down here to spend some time with Gareth, Peter's elder brother, and his family. Gordon has said he will come and pick you both up, and then take you home afterwards. Maddie and Gareth will be bringing their two boys, but Samantha, the baby of the family, wants to come in the car with me and Peter. Gordon will pick you and Uncle Donald up just before twelve which should be plenty of time to have a meal at around twelve thirty. Is that OK?'

'Looking forward to it' he replied.

29.

BRYN THOMAS HAD shared the results of the survey they had all been asked to undertake some months ago by the Department of Education and Science, with his Councillors in closed session. That arrangement was occasionally done when something was being discussed which they did not want the local press to know about until they were themselves more ready to deal with any awkward questions. On this occasion, the main reason for the discussions had been a report from the Department of Health into the performance of the main hospitals in the area. It made for depressing reading.

The Royal Gwent in Newport itself was now, apparently, amongst the bottom five in the whole country for performance against a whole host of central targets. Waiting times to be seen by a Consultant were now the longest in the whole of Wales by a considerable margin. There were now so many complaints about the standard of care – some from the individuals who had suffered (yes, he thought, there really was no other word which met the reality), but more often now by Lawyers acting on their behalf – that they could not literally be counted.

Nearly everyone in the room had had their own

experiences to relate, none of them supportive of their local hospital. When the Director of Health had said that there simply was no more money to throw at it in the hope of affecting some kind of improvement, there were howls of protest. Bryn himself had said loudly 'the statistics are quite damning, aren't they? There has to be an underlying reason, apart from money, that is at the root of the problem. The staffing levels are low, we can see that from the report, but they are no worse than the levels in existence in other places. We have a far larger number of staff, however, from areas outside the UK, particularly at the lower levels. Is that a part of the problem, perhaps even a major part?'

The Director had replied that they had to be careful that they were not accused of any form of racism with comments like that, but Bryn would have none of it. 'I'm talking about basic communication skills not race or creed or anything like it. Some of my neighbours who've been in the Gwent recently have said that an increasing number of staff who interact with the patients on the ward can barely speak, never mind understand, English. What must that be doing to the standard of care afforded to the patients?'

After a stormy debate lasting nearly two hours, the Director of Health was asked to come up with concrete proposals to improve the situation. He was given two weeks to do that. They would have to make the paper public knowledge after that, unless some 'investigative' reporter pre-empted that timescale. By that time the Chief Executive wanted to have some kind of plan ready to talk to the press.

Bryn's survey results had 'piggy-backed' onto the meeting and he was now asked to speak to it. When he outlined the results of the survey for the Gwent Council schools, there were gasps around the room.

'We knew there were difficulties in some parts of our area' the Chief Executive said, 'but I had no idea that our schools were performing quite so badly. To find that each of the village schools running up the Sirhowy Valley are all graded at the lowest level is really quite shocking.'

'Have you got anything else, any other information that might explain this dreadful situation?' the Director of Health demanded, clearly still smarting from the earlier discussion – and Bryn's part in it.

Bryn waved the full report covering the whole of the country above his head. 'This voluminous report has been compiled to cover the whole of the country' he said 'the part that you have had circulated only covers the final general assessments and the specific figures obtained from our area. I have only had a relatively short amount of time to assimilate the whole report, but it is already clear to me that there is a strong correlation between the school performance figures and the relative wealth of the areas being looked at. In our own area for example, not only does the Sirhowy valley fare badly but other areas such as Maindee and Duffryn do not do well either, while areas such as Langstone and Allt-Yr-Yn do well.'

'What does that mean then?' the Director of Health continued.

'It means to me that poor home environments lead to poor behaviour and then poor performance at school' Bryn replied.

'And have you any thoughts on how we can break into that vicious circle?' said the Chief Executive.

'I have one or two, but rather than try and discuss them in any depth here and now, I feel it would be wise to wait until after I've been to a meeting being organised in Bristol sometime in the next couple of weeks. The authors of the report are touring the country to talk to local Education Committees and try and find a way forward that everyone will agree on.'

'Keep us informed' was the final word on the issue by the Chief Executive before closing the meeting.

30.

MARTIN COOK HAD not come into politics to waste time. He still remembered all too clearly the embarrassment and then shame he had felt at the bullying he had suffered while at school. It had started, as far as he was ever able to make out, merely because he was a little smaller than the group of boys who felt it was fun to make someone cry. He had tried to tell his parents when it all started, but all his Mum could say was that he had to 'man up'. He had never had many friends while at his Primary School. The bigger boys had seen to that, frightening everyone away who might have wanted to play with him. If it hadn't been for Evan, he would have led a totally miserable existence. Evan wasn't able to do much about the bullying, but he would never really understand just how important it had been for Martin just to know that he wasn't completely alone.

On one occasion Martin had plucked up the courage to have a go back. It had resulted in a cut lip. But what made it all the more distressing for the little eight year old boy, was the fact that the teacher who was never around when it was happening to him, managed to see the retaliation. Being spoken to by the teacher and warned about his behaviour had given his tormentors even more ammunition. They knew that he would never come back at them again, no matter what they did to him. He cried himself to sleep on more than one occasion during that school year, and by the time he had left to join the Secondary School, he would not have recognised the term 'self worth'.

It had all left him with a burning desire to rid schools of that kind of behaviour. He wanted, more than anything else, to do something to make sure that no-one would ever have to go through the traumas he had suffered from that gang of bullies.

He had survived those years, somehow, but would never forget them. When he had spoken in Parliament in his earlier career, his impassioned speeches on school items which came before the house, had been no more than him speaking from the heart on a subject that he had very firm and clear views about.

Those speeches had not gone unnoticed. When the previous Minister for Schools had been 'moved on' he was asked to come into Government. The usual tittle tattle around the Palace of Westminster had it that the previous Minister had failed to stamp his authority on the job quickly enough. The Prime Minister had made it plain when he spoke to him before the appointment was made public, that he did not expect Martin to make the same mistake. It had been something of a surprise for him, but he quickly decided that it actually put him in a position where he might have a real say in how schools could and should manage their pupils better.

When he had first sat down behind the ornate desk which came with the title of Schools Minister, he had looked at his in tray in dismay. Ann Christie, Permanent Secretary in the department had come to welcome him shortly after he had arrived on that first morning and, pointing at the overflowing in tray, had said 'there's a lot going on in the Department as you will already have seen.'

Now, nearly a year later – good God, he said to himself at that thought, had it been a whole year ago already? – his in tray was just as full. One of the things he had not fully reckoned on was the sheer number of differing interests he had to deal with in this post. Teachers and their yearly complaints over salaries, complete with the usual strike threats, he had anticipated. What had not been in his mind was the plethora of difficulties arising over quite sensible improvements to the various age groups curricula. Differences in approach from the private and public sectors of the profession were plentiful, and yet needed to be reconciled so that a single Examination Board could assess pupils properly and consistently. He was beginning to wonder if he would ever be able to table proposals which would not unleash a storm of protests from teachers or other 'interest' groups somewhere.

He was also conscious that time was passing him by in his desire to make a difference to the Department's work. He knew that, if his political career was to continue upwards, he needed what used to be called 'the big idea' – some initiative that would forever link his name to progress in the

Department. As those thoughts flitted through his mind, he picked up the next item in his red box – the box of work that every Minister took home at night as visible proof that they worked on behalf of the great British public into the small hours at home after a busy day in Whitehall. One or two of his more senior colleagues laughingly referred to theirs as the most expensive lunch box you were ever likely to see.

Another paper on pupil behaviour in school. This one was a little more weighty than some of the others he had come across. When he started to read it, all the old memories came flooding back. This paper had been produced by the Departmental Standards and Testing Agency. Unusually, most of the recommendations they had made had already been supported by the Office of The Children's Commissioner and the National Association of Head Teachers, as well as the National Union of Teachers.

Essentially, what all of these bodies were saying was that the research reports' conclusions merely put facts onto a situation that they had all known was the picture on the ground. The behaviour of more and more pupils in schools had now reached the stage where it was clearly impacting on many other children there, and was showing up in falling school results in examinations. Bullying, and even downright physical abuse was on the rise. He had no difficulty relating to those conclusions.

The report had been compiled from data fed into it from an extensive survey carried out in the last six months via all Council Education Departments. When he looked below the major conclusions of the report to validate some of the data being examined, he was amazed at the disparity between Geographical areas. He was forcibly reminded of the old dictum that there were lies, damned lies and statistics.

While no-one had, as yet, made any comment about the disparity between geographical areas, it was apparent to Martin that they were there. Such areas as the London Boroughs of Tooting and Mitcham were clearly performing much less well than say Kensington and Knightsbridge. Outside of the big conurbations, there was a similar difference between areas in the north such as Gateshead and Harrogate, as well as South Wales and those living further north in the Principality. In all cases, it was apparent, at least to him, that poorer areas were suffering from a much higher incidence of bad behaviour to those in the more affluent ones. That was being fed through into exam results. So, he could see, a vicious circle of poor performance and poor behaviour was already in existence.

A footnote attached to one of the results from a teacher in Gateshead had said simply that there was a knock-on effect that needed to be addressed if any improvements were to be achieved. She had pointed out that, because of the problems in her area with pupil behaviour, she was finding it increasingly difficult to attract what she called quality teachers. Any who came into the area with some kind of ability, quickly found jobs elsewhere. The money was the same, with less hassle from pupils – and their parents. They had tried offering extra money to take on board the challenges of the area, without success. Something else, she had said, needed to be done.

As Martin read the report, the thought suddenly struck him again. Could this be the 'big idea' he had been looking for? Could this be the change that would light up his name in Parliament? Could this be what would boost his political influence into the stratosphere?

He knew there was a great deal of work to do before that could happen, but he also knew that he had waited long enough. It was time, he felt, for him to be noticed as more than just a rising star. He could become the heir apparent if this could be managed properly. As he poured himself another scotch and settled back into his armchair, he started to think.

31.

Bryn Thomas would never have described himself as a shrinking violet. When he had attended the meeting in Bristol yesterday, he had listened to all the others for what was to him quite a long time. They didn't half talk a load of bullshit though, and so he eventually decided enough was enough. It was time for someone to tell it like it was, not beat about the bush with their fancy words. The last speaker had been one too many for Bryn.

For a start he came from Clevedon, one of the wealthiest areas in the West Country, with one of the highest number of senior citizens. That meant that his local statistics were badly skewed from the rest of the area, and indeed the rest of the country. Prattling on about 'parental involvement in schools' and 'long term assessments' needing to be made before 'precipitate action' was taken, cut no ice with Bryn. He didn't think it cut much ice with the others either.

The Minister for Schools was in attendance, while one of the report's co-authors chaired the proceedings. That was a little unexpected, but as Martin Cook had said when he was being introduced, he felt the need to show an interest and this was not only the first of the planned programme of meetings, it was also one of the few being organised where his other responsibilities allowed him to come without undue changes to his own programme. Bryn thought that his attendance might also have served to mute some of the more critical comments being made. It did not faze Bryn, however. He had dealt with more important people than Martin Cook in his time.

'Isn't it about time that we – all of us – accepted that these figures, no matter how bad a picture of behaviour in our schools they paint, are facts?' Bryn said. 'Facts that we all need to take action about in order to improve not only behaviour in our schools, but the exam results which the facts outlined clearly show stem from the poor behaviour. This is the future generations we are talking about here. Generations which will only get one chance to develop and become useful members of society. We not only should do something about this, it is our absolute responsibility to do something.'

One of the other members said 'yes we can all agree with the sentiments Bryn, but the real difficulty is what in practical terms we can actually do about it?' Another one chimed in with 'we're already spending a substantial proportion of our budgets on counselling and support services for those children who seem to be the major cause of the problem.' There were a few heads nodding in agreement with that view, but Bryn would have none of it.

'Isn't it about time we recognised that those kinds of approach simply do not work? We have been employing Psychiatrists and Psychologists for a number of years and – I can only speak for my area – all they have achieved is to take a bigger and bigger cut from the Education budget, with damn all in the way of positive results to show for it.' There was uproar at this. Several of the others present started to shout that these were proven methods and they should not be dismissed so quickly.

Bryn rounded on them.

'How long do we need to wait for these so-called 'proven' methods to show some results? It is while these 'proven' methods have been getting used that we are now in this situation. From where I stand, we seem to have proven only that the 'proven' methods are useless in making real worthwhile changes. How long do the other children have to wait while these so-called 'professionals' practise on these kids, our kids. How long do the other kids have to put up with this abusive behaviour while it is ruining their own futures?' he demanded.

Martin Cook listened intently, not only to the words, but perhaps even more importantly, the mood of the meeting. Was this the window of opportunity he could use to push for that 'big idea' that he had in his mind? He knew that in these kinds of situations you had to strike while the iron was hot. 'I wonder' he said as the hubbub was dying down 'if there is room for an entirely new way of tackling what is clearly already a serious problem in our schools...'

'Some of them' a voice shouted from the middle of the hall.

'Yes, I suppose we have to take into account that the report does differentiate quite clearly between some geographical areas where the problems seem to be significantly worse. Nonetheless, as Bryn has said, our 'traditional' ways of looking at this issue would seem to be becoming less and less effective as time goes on. Perhaps an entirely new way of looking at these issues may be worthwhile.'

'What 'new way' are you talking about?' the Chairman said.

'Well, you all know that the use of drugs to modify behavioural patterns is already a well established methodology, particularly in the more difficult cases. I am aware from recent discussions within the Home Office that the use of – shall I call it a kind of vaccine – is currently being prepared for use in other areas of our troubled society where we are considering ways of permanently adjusting the perceptions of those who are a disruptive influence on the rest of society.'

'Are you saying that we should be giving all our children a vaccine of sorts to reduce their anti-social behaviour? That is a huge step away from our current practice isn't it?'

Martin said 'in some respects I agree that it is a change, but it might be no more than a slight change. We already – as a matter of course – provide vaccines for Flu, Meningitis and a number of other childhood complaints, don't we? It may be that all we are really talking about is another component in the mix of vaccines that are already supplied. It may be possible to have two types of vaccine, one with this new component for those children with behavioural problems and one we already supply to all schools. Is that so very different to the present system where those children with perceived behavioural problems get taken out of class to see specialists on a regular basis?

'What I see might be a future scenario would avoid children being removed from the classroom like that and reduce their feeling of being different. And, need I remind you, we have already established that the present regime of treatment has not and is not working effectively, haven't we? In those circumstances we would be remiss, wouldn't we, if we did not look at all possible alternatives? It is not my place, nor is this the venue to go into detail on those Home Office discussions, but we need to look at all ways, particularly non-violent ways, of improving the outlook of all members of our increasingly diverse society. It occurs to me that there might, just might, be value in looking into it for our own problem. If we can take steps to improve the attitudes of the youngest members of our society, we may at the same time be making huge inroads into potential future problems.'

The Chairman said 'whatever the detail of this new approach, it would need to be looked at very carefully and then trialled in one or two areas to test its efficacy, before we went to a full-blooded change in our procedures'.

Martin said 'of course we would need to observe all the normal precautions'.

One of the audience shouted 'if Bryn is so keen to see changes, perhaps you should use his area as the first area to try it all out. I don't think my Chief Executive would be too happy to be in the forefront of a change like this'.

Martin looked over at Bryn and said 'he has a point, doesn't he?'

Bryn could do nothing but agree.

32.

FRANK SUTHERLAND WAS, quite frankly, stunned. As he had listened to Hilary outlining the events of the day before, he had realised how vulnerable she had been. How vulnerable they all were in the face of the determination, long term planning and ruthlessness that people such as Ahmed Chisisi had shown. He was no expert on Islam, but he knew enough about the religion to know that the Quran spoke of Allah as being Beneficient and Merciful, in much the same way as the Jewish Tanakh, or the Christian Bible does. For groups such as these, it was quite unbelievable that they could hold human life in such disregard, while professing to hold to the Tenets of their faith. What had happened to Hilary so recently did not sit square with those ideals. But then, he said to himself, when did terrorism ever have any ideals other than terror?

He was amazed that Hilary had recovered so quickly from her ordeal. She was amazed herself, if the truth be known. She had listened yesterday to her Head of MI5 explain more of the background details of her encounter with the Terrorist group known as the African Brotherhood. She now understood a great deal more of how close she had come to death. The group were apparently well known in the Middle East as being one of the most ruthless operating there. Responsible for a number of terror attacks over recent years, they had been behind a particular suicide attack in a Cairo mosque.

Among those killed on that occasion had been the parents, wife and four year old son of Deniz Mehmet. When she had looked up enquiringly at that information, she was told that the man who had killed her would-be assassin was Deniz Mehmet. He had been working undercover in a specific attempt to get close to, and then 'take out' Ahmed Chisisi. Chisisi had not only masterminded a number of atrocities, he had been the main planner for that long ago outrage.

'Our colleagues in MI6 have been keeping in close contact with us about Chisisi, as one of many who we would have liked to 'interview' about a number of attacks on British personnel as well as Embassies in the Middle East. The security services had developed contacts in a number of those countries through a variety of agencies.

'We always hope that contacts like these will lead to prevention of activities rather than have to try and trace individuals after an event' he had said. 'Some we win, some we lose. This time we won, although only just. Mehmet was keeping in touch with his own controllers in Egypt electronically, but something as simple as a battery running down had caused that link to be less than perfect. As a result we were not able to trace them consistently after they landed by boat at a place called Kimmeridge Bay near Weymouth.'

'Did no-one see them land?'

'Apparently so Mam. There is a boathouse there and a small slipway. It is not always attended, being used mainly by weekend sailors and the like. One of the members of a sailing club which use the slipway regularly was however there making some repairs to his own boat. From what we now know, he saw them arrive. Unfortunately he did not survive the meeting to tell us what he saw. Mehmet's information was enough to show us where they had come ashore, and recover the man's body. His wife and two young children have been informed.'

'There were another four or five members of this group, I understand' Frank said. 'What happened there?'

'Mehmet didn't know where they were going to be living, but he knew that here – she allowed her eyes to rove around the Cabinet Office inside No10 – was where they intended to attack. He had been able to memorise the registration number of the vehicle they had been using for the pick up. The remainder of the group and some of their 'friends' who were already here in England, are being interviewed as we speak. We are still looking for others in the same terror cell. We will of course let you know what other intelligence we get as a result of those interviews, although it will take some time. People who were prepared to die in taking this kind of action are not the most cooperative of interviewees.'

'Well, I'm glad that you're safe anyway' Frank said.

'Yes, but it begs the question, doesn't it, about how we can take action to make this kind of thing much more difficult to achieve in future. From what I now know, the group – and you will not need to be told, there are many others with a similar purpose in mind – has clearly been planning this for a long time. Considerable resources were needed to get a boat and assemble a group of people who were quite prepared to make a long and dangerous journey and sacrifice their own lives in the hope that they could manage to get close enough to the British Government to cause havoc. Fanatical is the only word I can use, but I'm not sure it does justice to the threat these people clearly pose to our safety – ALL – our safety.'

'Why do I feel that you have some proposals in mind?'

'Yes, I do. We need to step up our patrols along the Channel significantly, and we need to do it now. This incident shows what can be done, and while not every group will have the resources to try something like this, many will try and make the much shorter sea crossing from Northern France toward our shores. We must be ready for them.'

'We've already agreed to bring the two carriers out of mothballs, haven't we?' Frank said.

'Yes, and they will be ready to move onto their stations within the next two weeks. What we need now – and this incident must show you how urgent it is – is for you to agree that we can start a programme of implants into those who will be processed there. We have the technology and we would look extremely foolish, perhaps even downright incompetent if something like this were to be repeated and we had passed up the chance to take effective action about it, wouldn't we?'

'I thought the last I heard from Eric Mercer, was that the software involved still need further development, before it was able to deliver?'

'There are still one or two bugs to be ironed out, but we can at least get the hardware implanted and then, when the software is ready to be used, we can be in a position to take effective action whenever we feel it is necessary. At the very least we will be able to keep track of people using this in the meantime, and in due course we will be able to modify individual behaviour as soon as the new software package is ready.'

'Yes, I see that. Let's do it. I'll tell Eric and then you can liaise with him over the details.'

'Thank you Prime Minister.'

33.

COLIN MCLEOD WAS looking forward to the meal with the family today. It would be nice to catch up with Rhona and also see Gordon Morrison after all this time. He knew that Donald had not been quite so happy when he was introduced to not just one, but two couples, who were clearly co-habiting. He had already known about Rhona and he had now discovered that Gordon Morrison and Rachel were in that same situation. They were blissfully happy, or at least they seemed to be, while Donald could only see the mortal sin involved.

Colin knew he would have to keep an eye on him otherwise he would 'say his piece' and be damned with the consequences. There had been some judicious placing of everyone at the start of the meal so that Donald had less opportunity to sound forth. Sitting between Maddie and her little girl Samantha had been a good idea. Maddie was of course safely – and happily, by all accounts – married to Gareth and Samantha was just a lovely little girl. For all their ability to find faults with the wider world, the Western Isles have always produced people who loved children.

* * * *

Sandra and James Wilson had almost decided not to make the effort to come out for a Sunday lunch. James eventually persuaded her that there was no value in ruining a weekend as well as suffering the stresses of a week at work. 'It'll be a good pick me up to go out and enjoy yourself for a few hours. Put school problems and paperwork behind you for a while'. She had agreed somewhat reluctantly. By the time James drew up outside the Maenllwyd Inn, she had to admit she was already feeling a little better.

As they both went inside, they could hear the chatter from all the other people. It raised Sandra's spirits a little more to see so many people enjoying themselves. The waiter had indicated they could use a table next to that occupied by one of the larger groups. As she passed by, she heard a voice say 'hello Mrs Wilson'. She turned and saw Madeleine Thomas along with what had to be a family party. 'Oh, hello' she replied.

Madeleine leant over as she and James were sitting down, and said, 'I hope we don't make too much noise for you.'

'Don't worry about it', Sandra said 'it's nice to see a big family gathering where everyone is enjoying themselves.'

Madeleine introduced her to the others, and Sandra said 'it's nice to come out like this when you have such a big family to share it with you.'

Peter Thomas said, 'yes, we don't get the chance to spend much time together. Rhona and I are normally in the South of England. In fact I think it's been a very long time since we were all together.'

Nathan said 'Grandad is the only one who isn't here isn't he Mum?'

Madeleine smiled and said 'yes he was too busy to come, as usual. You might have met him before', she said turning to Sally. 'He's the new Chair of the Education Committee at Newport Council.'

Sandra could feel the colour draining from her face. 'You mean Bryn Thomas?' she said incredulously.

'Yes.'

'I had no idea there was a connection. Thomas is a very common name around these parts, but still I should perhaps have wondered.' By this time both Gareth and Peter were taking an interest.

Peter said 'it doesn't look as if any contact you might have already made has been a pleasant one?'

'That is putting it mildly' she replied.

'Would you like to tell us a little bit more?' Gareth said as he went up to the bar with Sandra and Peter.

Meanwhile Colin and Donald were holding forth on the proceedings they were involved in at the Conference. 'There seems to be no understanding of parental responsibility anymore' Donald was saying to the rest of them.

'To be honest Uncle Donald' Rhona said 'it's one of the main reasons why Peter and I have stopped short at marriage.' Donald made to interject – until Colin pressed on his foot under the table – hard.

'Why is that Rhona' Colin asked.

'Well, we both feel that children should be brought up

in a caring and supportive environment. When we've visited friends in our neck of the woods, that is something that is nearly always missing. Too many parents these days seem to think that, once they've tied the knot, that is all they need to do. Children are seen by far too many in the South East as some kind of 'fashion accessory' rather than an expression of how much the adults are in a relationship where they care for each other and how much they want to bring others into a world where they can share the same sense of commitment to others.'

'Does Peter feel the same way?' Colin asked.

'You can ask him if you want, but be ready for a long discussion on how society today has lost its way.'

'Seems like Peter has views not so very far removed from our own, eh, Donald?' Colin said. Donald nodded in silence.

* * * *

While Gareth was ordering the drinks from the bar, Peter started what he thought was going to be a casual conversation with Sandra. 'So you've met our dearly beloved father, have you? If our experiences are anything to go by, we can both well understand why it might not have been a pleasant encounter. Bryn Thomas prides himself on controlling everything and everyone around him.'

'He's certainly trying to do that in his new job. But he is very heavy handed about it.'

'Yes' Peter said 'tact was never one of his strong points.'

'Apart from trying to ride rough shod over any point of view that is different to his own, he seems to be pursuing some kind of agenda that is making me feel quite nervous.'

'Like what?'

'Like talking – loudly and all the time – about the need to change pupil's behaviour. He has said at more than one meeting that the area is getting a bad name for it and he will do whatever is necessary to change things.'

'Has he gone into any details?' Gareth chimed in as he turned round with the tray of drinks.

'The last time he was sounding off, he said that Psychologists and psychiatrists have had their chance and it was clear that even with the drugs they sometimes used, they had shown themselves to be largely useless in making significant changes to pupil behaviour. We now need to do something else, something that would be much more effective. He did mutter something about some research into a new way of doing things which people 'in high places' were considering. He didn't answer when someone asked where and when this would all be taking place, but I got the impression that it was something that was likely to happen in the relatively near future.'

Peter felt as if someone had poured a bucket of cold water over him. Was it possible that somehow his research was being talked about in areas that he had never considered? He had never fully thought this through, but of course the Department was now known as the Department of

EDUCATION and Science. Was one, perhaps more than one, of their political masters looking at his research from a very different perspective?

* * * *

When Gareth returned from the bar, he found that the seating arrangement had been changed. He was now sandwiched between Gordon Morrison and his girlfriend and the two boys. It didn't take long for the two men to discover a shared interest in boats. As Gordon described his new pride and joy, Gareth could see the boys' eyes widening. He had always enjoyed the time he had spent with his own Bampie who had a boat moored at Swansea Marina. He had never been able to afford one of this own, but he had regaled the boys from time to time about the fun he had had on board a boat at weekends when he was much younger. When he told Gordon about that, Gordon leaned over to Nathan and Daniel and said 'would you like to come up to our place sometime soon and your dad and I will take you out on my boat?'

Their eyes were like saucers. 'Do you really mean that?' Nathan said.

'Of course I do' Gordon replied. I'll sort something out with your dad before we leave here today.

'Cool' was the response, and Gareth and Gordon both laughed.

34.

As Eric Mercer walked the short distance along the corridor of the Home Office building, he wondered what he was going to find. He had heard (who in Whitehall hadn't?) about the episode at Hilary Watson's weekend home. That had led to all kinds of security officers sweeping his own house set in the village of Freckenham, some five miles outside of the bigger and more famous East Anglian town of Newmarket. His wife was not best pleased at the changes they were now putting in place, but he knew they were only doing their job. A job which this time was focused on making sure that he and his wife were safer than had previously been the case. He certainly was not going to remonstrate with them, even when one of them had dragged a ladder right through the middle of Myra's prize Dahlia's.

He still expected Hilary to be quite traumatised – he knew he would have been – at what had happened, and what might so easily have been a different outcome. They had already talked about deploying ships in the channel and using those two aircraft carriers as staging posts for some of those who wanted to come here, and were prepared to risk anything to achieve that objective. What had so nearly happened to Hilary had been a real wake-up call for all the members of the Cabinet.

He was surprised when he went in, to see her much the same as normal. Maybe some of those stories which circulated between private offices weren't so wide of the mark, after all. He had heard that some felt she was a hard bitch, some had even said that she 'batted for the other side'. He'd never paid much attention to scuttlebut like that. For him, the only criteria that was important, was the way she carried out her job. So far, he felt she was firm, but not unreasonably hard. As far as the other thing was concerned, even if it were true, it was her business, as long as she didn't bring it into the office.

He said as he came up to the coffee table which already had cups on it 'glad to see you looking so well'. She merely nodded and then got straight into the business of the meeting. 'Eric, we are going ahead with the idea of using implants on those who come ashore after being 'processed'. I've spoken to the PM and he has agreed.'

'He hasn't said anything to me yet' Eric protested.

'Trust me, he will.' She replied. 'Anyway, I – WE – now need to press ahead with all speed. We've been told from some of our intelligence 'contacts' that there are several boatloads getting ready in Northern France right now and will shortly be setting out to cross the Channel. There is also a clear indication that there are at least two other groups such as the ones intercepted on this occasion who are already in the country. The security services have already ascertained as much from the interviews with members of the second group who were aiming for action in Downing Street itself. They have apparently entered the country recently through a variety of different routes and are making whatever plans they have. While we don't have the detail of those as yet, you can be sure they are not aimed at the welfare of the British people.

We are now looking for them as a matter of urgency, but information about where they may be is sketchy to say the least. That is because we have not been able to track them down with any accuracy. If we had been able to have the new technology in place, even in its imperfect state, we would have been in a better position to act against them rather than wait and play catch up.

I'm ordering today the requisitioning of several of the more modern vessels tied up in a number of South Coast marinas. A mixture of Coastguard staff and Royal Navy personnel will man these for the foreseeable future. You need to crack on with the production of the implants so that they can be used as part of the medical examinations – much as we previously discussed.'

'You will remember, Hilary, that I warned against moving too fast with this. The software is not ready to be used like this, yet. Have you thought about the actual practicalities of doing the implants? Who is actually going to have to do this, and are they happy with the ethical considerations? Have you thought through how we are to explain this new procedure to others who will be only too ready to scream 'civil liberties' once this becomes public knowledge, as it undoubtedly will? This is far too big an issue for a knee jerk reaction.'

'Look Eric, the PM agrees that we are going to do this. It is about time we stopped worrying so much about 'ethics' and concentrated more on 'safety' – safety for us in Government and safety for the population at large. We will not be easily forgiven if the next atrocity kills women and children, perhaps in large numbers in a Shopping Mall for example, or some other public place and it comes to light that we – you and I – had the means to have prevented it and we did nothing? As for those who will carry out the injections, that will be done by military medical personnel as part of their normal medical examinations on board the ships we will be using to process these prospective immigrants. They will be acting under strict military orders. I don't think we will have much problem there.

'The PM agrees with me that we will need to conduct the final trials of the software effectiveness after the implants are installed. For now, the task is to get production moving, and moving as fast as possible. You do not need me to remind you that the group who visited me had colleagues who were planning to make Downing Street their next target. Having been thwarted as they were, our intelligence sources are adamant that we can expect something else – and pretty soon. The publicity over their failed attempt will have ensured that they will try and make amends, if for no other reason than to reassert their position with other terrorists. In the short term, the implants will enable us to keep tabs on their whereabouts and, in due course, prevent a possible bloodbath on the streets of London. Needless to say, such an event would have its effect on the outcome of the next General Election, wouldn't it?'

* * * *

Colin McLeod thought that it had been a wonderful afternoon, as he sat back and sipped his second glass of orange juice, while the waitress cleared the stacks of empty – sometimes half empty! – plates which told of the end of a meal at the Maenllwyd Inn. He had spent a lot of time with the two boys as well as Samantha, as had Donald. They were now being affectionately known to the three children as Uncle Donald and Uncle Colin. He had to admit he hadn't seen Donald quite so happy and relaxed in a long time.

The two boys had been very well-behaved, even Donald had remarked on it and said they were very polite and a credit to their parents. Donald had actually gone as far as to say that they were as well brought up as any he had ever met from home. That was a huge compliment in Donald's eyes. They had now been given permission to take their little sister outside for a few minutes to play on the swings in the garden. As the three youngsters ran outside, the two brothers exchanged smiles and then turned their attention to the rest of the group.

Sandra was by this time quite agitated. Colin said 'would you like to bring us up to speed on what the discussion is all about? It's fairly obvious that Mrs Wilson at least is quite upset at whatever it is.' Peter and Gareth were quick to give the brothers a short history, not only of family relationships over the years, but also a picture of the bare bones of what they had been talking to Sandra about.

When they had finished, there was a general hubbub of talk from the others, all wanting to express their disgust at what was being said.

'Do you really believe this is possible?' said Donald.

'I'm afraid our experiences since early childhood tell us that it fits very well with what we know about our father.' Peter said. 'What Gareth and I don't know is what it might mean in practical terms and what the view from the centre is'. He looked at Gareth and got a nod in return.

'Is there any way you can verify this?' Donald continued.

'As soon as I get back tomorrow, you can be sure I will be asking some very awkward questions. I know it won't make me very popular in the corridors of power, but I'm fast reaching the conclusion that I don't really care about them any more. He looked questioningly over to Gareth. The smile of encouragement he got in return was all he needed.

The drive back to their house in Cwmfelinfach was a quiet one for Gareth and Maddie. Each was lost in their own thoughts. It wasn't until the three children were safely upstairs, that they felt free to say anything about what they had been hearing. It was Maddie who broke the silence.

'Are you going to talk to Bryn?' she said.

'I don't suppose I have much option, but I don't think it will get us anywhere. You know what he is like.

'What do we do, if it turns out to be true?'

'That is a more difficult question. Maybe we shouldn't jump down that road until we know for certain that is what we are faced with.'

'But you will speak to him?' Maddie pressed, realising that it would inevitably be a very difficult conversation.

'Yes.'

35.

GARETH WASN'T LOOKING forward to the conversation he knew he was going to have with his father. Maddie had made it crystal clear about what she felt needed to be said and, on this occasion, Gareth agreed completely with her views. He had sometimes tried to water down her reactions to Bryn, feeling that, well, they were family after all. He instinctively felt that they should 'give' a little more than Maddie often wanted. This time, however, he was if anything even more incensed with what seemed to be going on. The thought that his own father might be heavily involved in it, was just a whole step too far for the normally mild mannered Gareth.

When he got into the Garage Office on the Monday, he rather hoped Bryn wouldn't be there. Although he was ready for the confrontation, he was still reluctant to start the conversation when he knew deep down where it was likely to end. Monday was always Gareth's busiest day of the week. He had work already booked of course, but that was the day when every man and his dog seemed to ring up to arrange more. He was, nevertheless, about to give his father a ring and find out when he was coming in, when he heard the iPad he always carried with him 'ping' to denote that a message had arrived. He sat down to see who wanted him so early on Monday. Probably one of his older customers whose car had given up the ghost again over the weekend. He was a little surprised to see Bryn's name at the top of the incoming message. 'En route to important Council business in London today and Tuesday. Will see you sometime Wednesday.

* * * *

It had become a bit of a habit for Hilary Watson to have her evening meal prepared by Sally Thomas when she got home to her house in Four Marks at the weekend. Sally was really a gem, she thought. There had been occasions when she had been very late indeed if there was business in the House which had overtaken her.

She had managed to get home at a more civilised hour this time and Sally was still there putting the finishing touches to the Boeuf Bourguignon she had prepared. She prattled on as she got it ready to put it on the table about the big event she was going to at St Lawrence Church in nearby Alton on the Saturday. Apparently the new Bishop of Winchester was coming to the Church to open some joint event being run by the four churches in the town. It was, she said, part of the GAP project.

Hilary said 'the GAP project? What is that? I've never heard of it.' Sally explained that it was an effort by all the churches in the Alton area to work more closely together, for the benefit of the whole community. They were hoping to bring the Anglican and Methodist churches much closer together. She was looking forward to meeting the new Bishop. She had been given the job of coordinating all their efforts for this event when the idea was first put forward. Getting them all to cooperate had not been easy, she said and Hilary replied 'a bit like politicians then eh?' and they had both laughed.

It was no more than nine o'clock when she finished the meal, put the dishes in the dishwasher and went through to the lounge with a glass of wine. She looked with distaste at the red box perched threateningly on the coffee table. Should she open it tonight? No, to hell with it, tomorrow would do. Tonight she would relax and have some time to herself, rather than always dealing with other people's problems.

She had barely filled her glass for the second time and put some relaxing music on – something by Brahms or Chopin that was a new Classical CD which Sally – God bless her! – had left for her to listen to, when the phone rang. Damn! She thought. Can't I even get one night without interruption and at a weekend too? Then she remembered what had happened in this very lounge so recently and wondered if it might be someone from the security services checking she was alright. If she didn't answer, she might find another set of boots coming in through the front window in a few minutes!

When she lifted the phone, she didn't recognise the voice. Martin Cook had to say who he was, and remind her of some of the meetings they had recently attended together. She did say eventually, that perhaps she hadn't recognised his voice, because she wasn't sure she had heard him speak at those meetings. He laughed and said 'I think you may be right. I've adopted an approach that says keep quiet unless or until you have something sensible to say that others might want to hear.' She smiled as she said 'that's not a bad approach, although it is unusual to find it amongst a group of politicians. Anyway, what can I do for you this Friday night?'

There was just enough emphasis on the 'Friday' for Martin to recognise that she was at best not pleased at this invasion into her free time. He said 'I'm sorry to interfere with your weekend like this, but I am travelling down to Southampton tomorrow morning to speak to a group of Head Teachers in the area. They're at the end of a two day seminar discussing common problems, and in particular the ongoing and increasing concerns about pupil behaviour. I've been asked to come and take part in a question and answer session with them at the conclusion of their debates.'

'All very interesting, Martin' Hilary said 'but how does this involve me?'

'Well, one of the meetings I attended with you and Eric Mercer recently was considering a new method of affecting suspected terrorists'/immigrants' behaviour. It came up as part of a discussion that was going on about treatment for Alzheimer's if I recall correctly. As I understood it, it was based around some kind of injection – I think Eric referred to it as an implant – and then using what to me was highly sophisticated software to access Neurons in the brain functions which would allow someone to modify brain patterns and through them, individual behaviours in anyone who had been given the injection.' Have I got that right?

'Yes'

'Well, I wanted to talk to someone about how this technology might be transferred elsewhere in society.'

'Shouldn't you be having this conversation with Eric?'

'I suppose so, but I felt it was better to bounce my first feelings off someone who might have a more positive outlook. Eric is my Minister, but he does tend to always take a negative stance on anything which is radically new.'

'So, what do you want me to do about it?'

'I was hoping that as I was passing your door tomorrow as it were, you might be able to find some time to run through my ideas. I'm prepared to accept that I'm wildly out in terms of a practical application with what I'm thinking, but I need to hear that from someone whose approach is a little closer to mine than I fear Eric's is. He is likely to find all the negatives and not want to see the positives. I'm hoping, from what I heard from you during those meetings, that you might be more prepared to look at the ideas more dispassionately.'

Hilary had always been ready to look at new concepts, especially when they might fit in with her own goals. If Martin Cook had come up with something else where this new technology would prove useful, it gave even more credence to her approach over the immigration issue. If it wasn't such a good idea she could always use any rejection of it as a platform to deflect possible later criticism that she had rushed into her own efforts without careful thought.

On balance she felt it would be a good idea to listen to what Martin Cook had to say. They swiftly arranged that she would make herself available from around three o'clock the next afternoon. That would, he said, fit in very well with the timing of his meeting in Southampton.

36.

WHEN COLIN SAT down on the plane for the first leg of the trip home with Donald, he was looking for a pleasant, quiet journey home after what had been a successful few days. He had found the fringe meetings he had attended to be very worthwhile with a number of new perspectives provided by the members on the difficulties they had encountered trying to infuse younger members in their respective congregations with the same enthusiasm they felt themselves. Donald's keynote speech had been well received too, and the members of the wider movement had agreed to take the views expressed there back to their own churches. They were both pleased that they had agreed to come and take part in the Conference.

As the plane lifted off the tarmac at Cardiff airport, Donald turned to him and said

'What did you think of it all then, brother?'

'Your speech went down very well' Colin replied. 'I'm sure James will be very pleased to hear our reports when we get home.'

'I was thinking more about your discussion group. How did you get on with the V.I.P.?'

'He turned out to be very different to what you might

expect. Very down to Earth. We found ourselves on the same side of the discussions most of the time. I've even got his personal phone number. He said I should call him if I was ever down in his area and he would arrange for us to have a meal together and have an opportunity to discuss our joint views a little further.'

'Seems like you did your bit for bringing the Churches closer together then, eh? James will be pleased when we tell him. How about the Sunday lunch? I thought that it went quite well.'

'Yes, it did. I thought it was really good to make contact with Rhona again. It's been a while, hasn't it?'

'Yes, and Peter seems like a nice sort, even if he has still to tie the knot with Rhona. The rest of his family were extremely pleasant and polite too. It was quite disturbing to hear that Head Teacher and what she had to say, though.'

'If even half of it is accurate, it will be positively dreadful. Makes you glad we live well away from those kind of things doesn't it? There's not a lot we can do about it to help though is there?'

'I've been thinking about that a little over the rest of the weekend, actually.' Donald went on. 'We should perhaps invite them all to come up to us for a holiday or something. We could let them see how the other half lives or something like that. You've got plenty of space in that house of yours. I sometimes wonder how you like rattling around in there all by yourself. Mum would also love to put some of the others up for a visit, particularly the little girl, Samantha. I know it won't solve their problems, if indeed there is a real problem, but it might give them a wider view of how things could be, and help them to argue against a proposal that seems quite ridiculous and very high handed. At the very least it gives us a chance to keep the contact going. They are a nice family and Samantha is just a sweet little girl, isn't she? What do you think?'

Colin was amazed. This usually very gruff and outspoken brother of his was downright smitten by a little girl! It was true, however, she was a gem, and very well behaved and polite, as indeed the whole family was, and anything that brought his sometime harsh speaking brother back nearer to the gentle world that lay beneath the rough exterior, was something that he would always encourage. 'I think that's an excellent idea, Donald. The next time I'm on the phone to Rhona I'll suggest that.'

* * * *

37.

IT WAS A BEAUTIFUL Saturday afternoon when Martin Cook knocked on the door of Hilary Watson's house down the tree lined avenue that was Blackberry Lane in the village of Four Marks in the north of Hampshire. Hilary took him out into the back garden where she had tea and sandwiches prepared. As he sat down and looked at the manicured lawn, he turned to her and said 'this is really quite a superb garden.'

'I have a couple nearby who do most of the work. Sally does a sterling job not only looking after the house but acting as a secretary for me during the week, and her partner – Walter – does the same for the garden. It's his handiwork you see here, not mine.'

'Nevertheless it is quite lovely', he said.

'I felt it was a good idea to discuss this idea of yours out here. You never know what security devices, including microphones, there might be inside.'

That thought had clearly never occurred to Martin, as he looked back at the house they had just left.

Sitting down, Hilary said 'now what can I do for you that your own Minister would not have liked?'

* * * *

When Martin Cook had finished explaining what he saw as the way forward to curb school behaviour, Hilary Watson sat back. It would have been easy to ridicule his ideas, they were after all quite revolutionary, as he himself had admitted. She could also see why he had not wanted the first Ministerial discussion on the subject to be with Eric Mercer. Eric, she had decided a long time ago, was what was still called 'a safe pair of hands' or sometimes even 'an old woman' particularly where new ideas were being brought forward. What both euphemisms said was that he – and others like him – avoided putting any new ideas into practice. Doing so involved taking risks, and some Ministers, Eric included, were just, well, too comfortable in their post to want anything to happen which might lead to them losing that position. She had learned a long time ago that, to men like that, 'no' is nearly always a safer option than 'yes'.

She had never experienced much in the way of anti-social behaviour at school. The Malvern School had been fee paying, as all of her schools had been, and that fact alone was enough to prevent what the Head Teacher there had always referred to as 'the riff-raff' from attending with their big mouths and small minds. She had, however, heard from many of her constituents during her time in Parliament that the standards of behaviour in schools were steadily dropping. Parents had, on occasion, been quite distressed by what was happening to their children at the hands of others who were more concerned with the latest computerised game or the smart watches they all now sported from a very early age, than with fostering real relationships. It hadn't, she thought wryly, stopped them from buying the damned things themselves though, had it? This disconnection with other children had meant that many no longer knew how to interact sensibly with others. Perhaps, she thought, didn't care might be a more appropriate way of describing it.

Until Martin had outlined the nature of the discussion he had just held with Head Teachers in the Southampton area and also explained that the recent survey was saying much the same thing, she had felt it was all something that she only needed to be vaguely aware of. In her eyes it had been something purely for the Department of Education to get on with. She had bigger fish to fry. Now she wasn't so sure.

It was, after all, one thing for problems to be dealt with in terms of Schools by the Minister for Education and Science. That was entirely proper and was no business of hers. However, as Martin had just laid out very comprehensively in front of her, there was an unsavoury future waiting for them all if this problem was not dealt with at the school level – and the primary stage at that. The results of the latest examinations are what had prompted the review of results throughout the country to be made. Those results did not make for pleasant reading.

What Martin had been at pains to explain, was the consequences for the whole of society if poorly taught and largely uneducated streams of children were to become the norm. The behaviour of children at school was quite clearly highlighted in the report as the major cause for this failing. In turn, that failing was likely to deliver a future for the whole country that no-one in Government would be happy about.

In Martin's own words, 'Unruly behaviour at Primary ages often becomes criminal behaviour as an adult – the link is clear. Correcting that behaviour at the earliest opportunity, by whatever means available, will lead to less criminal behaviour later on. The obvious later benefit to society as a whole should be obvious and must be our focus.'

In these circumstances, the issue went way outside the remit of Education and Science alone and was, arguably, a major issue for everyone in the Cabinet. What Martin had suggested as a course of action to tackle the problem was still extreme, but maybe, she thought, just maybe, it would be the best way forward. She knew that introducing the idea to colleagues in the Cabinet was fraught with danger. They were after all known as the Conservative party and that was for a reason. There were some who paid more than lip service to the idea of 'civil liberties' and they would join with the others who disliked the idea of children being the subject of trials of this nature.

She, on the other hand, subscribed to the idea that as Civilisation progressed, it was inevitable that personal privacy would diminish. CCTV cameras on motorways and then in town centres were all old technology and the end of the world had not materialised with their introduction. The internet and the ability to listen in to others' conversations across the ether was merely seen as a further stage in that process.

The plans already underway for curtailing terrorists and indeed prisoners out on licence took us further down the same road. What Martin was suggesting was different but was essentially heading down the same path. Yes, she thought, it would be difficult to get these ideas past Cabinet. Difficult, but not impossible.

'What are your plans for the rest of the evening, Martin?' she enquired.

'I don't have anything planned. I didn't know how long I might spend here, and so I intended to drive back to my flat in London, and then think about eating.'

'Why don't you have a meal here and we can go over some of your ideas again. I may need to get involved in this myself, and I'd better be a bit more clued up on some of the basics before I do. While we're together like this, it might be sensible to go over not only the plus points in this idea of yours, but also examine where we are likely to meet opposition if we decide to take it all further. Why don't we arrange for a Chinese takeaway from the shop in the village? They're normally very good, and we can discuss the matter while we eat?' This is a big house and I have more than one bedroom which is normally unused. Why don't we take the opportunity to explore the idea further with a couple of glasses of wine?

'Fine by me Hilary' Martin said. 'Will I be able to pick

up a bottle of wine somewhere nearby when I go for the Chinese?'

'Don't worry about that, Martin. I have a couple of bottles of very nice Pinot Grigio in the garage. They'll do the job nicely, I think.'

38.

SALLY THOMAS WAS having difficulty breathing. She had come in on the Tuesday morning to open Hilary's post as she normally did. They had agreed that there was no real need to do so on a Monday as Hilary would have been there all weekend and would have cleared all the outstanding mail. Any urgent stuff would be picked up and sent out immediately by either fax or e-mail to Hilary's Private Office in Westminster.

The last envelope she had opened had looked ordinary enough. When she read the contents, it took a few moments for their import to sink in. It was a note from a Martin Cook, someone she had never met, but someone who was clearly well placed in Government circles. In it he summarised a discussion which he had had with Hilary. She could barely believe the words she was reading. Were they really going to try and change pupil behaviour by giving injections to all children? She had not had a whiff of anything like that from reading Hilary's post over the last few months, but it looked as if it was something that was going to be put in place soon – very soon. She could imagine the reaction to that when parents got to hear about it. She wasn't too happy at the thought of her own grandchildren being subjected to something like that.

She decided that, although it was against all the rules Hilary had made for her treatment of mail, this was too big to ignore. Although she didn't know any details (she probably wouldn't have understood them anyway) her son Peter, she knew, was doing some kind of Government research locally. Maybe she should give him a call and see if he knew anything about it.

* * * *

39.

PETER HAD BEEN exceptionally busy on the Monday after he had driven back down from South Wales. So busy in fact that he had not been able to get an opportunity to see Arnold. He must make sure, he thought, that tomorrow did not go the same way.

Rhona was at home by the time he pulled into their driveway. As soon as he came into the lounge, she said

'You're Mum has been on the phone. She wants to speak to you and it sounded urgent.'

'Did she say what it was about?'

'No, but when I looked at our answering machine it has been the fourth time she has tried to speak to you today.'

'OK, I'll give her a ring as soon as I get changed.'

He didn't get a chance. Rhona and he didn't drink very much, but they had got into the habit of having a small vodka mixed with Coca Cola while they were preparing their evening meal. Rhona had been saying for the last few weeks that she intended to cut even that out as she felt it was best for their future plans. He didn't need to think what those might be. The recent visits to South Wales and a precocious little girl had shown him where Rhona's thoughts were.

When he came back downstairs, he was just about to pour her an orange juice, when the phone rang. It was his mother. 'Hi Mother' he said. 'Rhona has just been telling me that you have been trying to get in touch. Is there anything the matter?'

'I'm not really sure' she said. 'But I need to tell you something and then let you decide.'

* * * *

After his mother had finished explaining about the note she had opened in Hilary Watson's post, Peter knew his worst fears were being realised.

'Do you know these people, Peter?' his mother asked. 'All I know is that Hilary, the woman that I occasionally work for, is the Home Secretary.'

'Martin Cook is the Minister for Schools within my own Department, he reports to Eric Mercer who is the Minister for Education and Science.'

'So this Martin Cook will have some kind of responsibility for doing something like this?' she asked.

'Yes, Mother, it will be part of his remit to oversee matters affecting schools in England. Unfortunately, the way things are still organised, it means that he will also be responsible for much of what happens in Wales too. Common examinations standards still apply to both areas, not like Scotland where they have a different set of exams. Were you aware that dad has recently been made Chairman of the Education Committee for Newport Council?'

Sally did a double take.

'Are you trying to tell me that he might be involved in all this too?'

'I don't yet know that for certain and if so, to what extent, but I intend to find out.'

* * * *

40.

As MARTIN COOK walked the short distance along the corridor to Eric Mercer's room, he felt quietly pleased that he had made that initial contact with Hilary Watson. He was pretty certain that if he had raised his idea directly with Eric, before speaking to anyone else, it might never have seen the light of day. The world according to Westminster was, of course, full of leaks and irrational rumours. It would nevertheless have put him in a bad light if he had tried to continue with the proposal to modify the procedure intended for potential terrorists, if his own Minister had already ruled it out. Nothing was quite as serious as disloyalty to a politician. The subject matter was of no consequence when someone had bypassed instructions from his political senior and attempted to get his own way in spite of their views. The possible benefits to be gained by using this approach would have been lost in the outcry directed at him.

In true Civil Service fashion, he had followed up the discussions he had had with Hilary by writing her a personal note. It helped him to get the ideas clearer in his own head and provided insurance for him if things went wrong somehow. It would do no harm in that unlikely turn of events to be able to point to the fact that he had written to a senior member of the Cabinet outlining what he proposed before taking any action. That placed the responsibility on her, rather than his, shoulders.

Hilary had already more or less decided that there was merit in the use of the vaccine. He was aware that term was not strictly correct, but it sounded better than the bald term injection. When he had outlined the mood of the meeting in Bristol, she felt as he did that it was an opportunity that should not be missed. What was needed was to bring Eric Mercer on board. As the relevant Minister, any proposals such as this would have to come from him.

As he entered the room, Hilary was just sitting back having said some of her piece to Eric. He was looking distinctly unhappy. He turned to Martin and said 'you might have come to me with this, before bringing Hilary in on it.'

'I'm sorry Eric' Martin said 'but I'm sure Hilary told you that it was pure co-incidence that we crossed each others paths almost immediately I had left the weekend meeting in Southampton. You remember, the one that you said you were too busy to attend.' He didn't say that their paths had crossed because both Hilary and he had agreed that they should.

'Well there are principles as well as practicalities here' Eric went on. 'For a start, we cannot just go around giving injections to children unless there is a very good reason to do so, and we would even then have to agree procedures with all sorts of bodies who have a vested interest. Local Health authorities as well as Council Education Committees would all have to be onside before we could do anything like this.'

'Yes I know Eric' Martin said 'but we already know from the mood of that first meeting – a mood may I say that I'm told has been reflected almost exactly in the other meetings that have been held since – that a great number of those who might be involved are ready to see some kind of radical change in the way we try and help these problem children become worthwhile members of a future society. In terms of the practicalities, we already have an ongoing programme of medical examinations at several points in a child's school life. There will be no separate examinations for this implant. It will merely be administered at the same time as the usual round of vaccinations against meningitis et al.

Eric didn't look particularly convinced by that argument, but he continued 'but we barely have enough material to cater for the needs of the Home Office to use in their Immigration programme.' He looked at Hilary accusingly.

'That may be true at the moment, but that situation will improve as production gather pace' she said. 'In any case, we are not talking about changing these procedures in the next few weeks, are we? Apart from any discussions we might need to have here, we need to set up some kind of trial out in the sticks, so that you can eventually take it all to Cabinet and demonstrate its effectiveness – at least that is the plan, isn't it?' she said looking at Martin. He came in smoothly.

'When I attended the meeting in Bristol, one of the Education Chairmen spoke at some length about the need to do something more concrete than just continue the same way we had done for a number of years now. His area was one of those which had shown the lowest set of marks in recent examinations and therefore had the greatest potential for improvement if we used his area as one of the trial projects. There was no mileage, he said, in merely throwing more money at the problem. One of the other members from the floor actually said that if he was so keen to change things maybe he should try it in his own area first before lecturing everyone else.'

'So Martin here' interjected Hilary 'feels that there would be merit in doing exactly that. It would make every kind of sense to trial the new way in one or perhaps two areas and see how it goes.

We can't start it all up right away of course. We need to get someone at each location trained up so that they can use the software to make the necessary modifications to those who show antisocial behaviour frequently. Each of the schools has a 'special needs' teacher, and we need to see whether that is the best place to have the new procedure managed from. It may be that the precise 'how' will vary from school to school. That is after all one of the purposes of a trial like this isn't it?

'If it is a success then we can bring it forward as a ready made answer to a problem that we all know is exercising parents groups right across the country and the political spectrum.'

'And if it isn't a success?' Eric queried.

''Then we have at least tried' Martin replied. 'Peter Thomas's research has at least demonstrated quite conclusively that there are no noticeable side effects to the treatment. If we just have to leave the implant in place and never make use of it as we would like, and then move onto a different approach, no-one will have been disadvantaged, or hurt.'

They could both see that Eric was still doubtful of the approach being suggested, but couldn't mount a coherent argument against it. He made one last try.

'Shouldn't we run this by Frank before we put this trial in place?'

'I've already covered that ground with him in relation to the Immigration system, haven't I?' Hilary said. 'I don't think he would thank us for wasting his time going over what is essentially old ground, especially when he is so busy with the latest trade negotiations with U.S.A. Leaving the Common Market , the way we had to when we left the EU has, as you well know meant a great deal of energy has to be expended in tying down alternative trade deals. He has made it clear in recent cabinet discussions that those potential deals with the USA are his number one priority just now, hasn't he?'

Eric was beaten, and he knew it. Like all good politicians, however, he still wanted to cover his back. 'If you are both telling me that this is a trial that you feel has a good chance of success, then I will run with it. I'll note the record of this meeting to that effect, shall I?'

Hilary and Martin merely exchanged looks and a smile.

41.

BRYN THOMAS HADN'T been on a train for many years. When he was asked by Martin Cook – the Minister for Schools no less, he said to himself, asking for me by name – to come to London to take part in discussions following the series of meetings held around the country to debate the survey of behaviour, he was ecstatic. Now he was beginning to move in those circles he thought were truly important. He hadn't relished the idea of driving into the capital, although he would never have admitted that to anyone. Martin's offer of either a reserved space in the Departmental car park, or a first class rail ticket and his expenses, gave him the way out he would have tried to achieve anyway. 'Train seems the best way, Minister', he had said 'that way I can read over the conclusions of the survey again and be ready to talk as soon as I get in.'

Martin had said to him that they intended to run over a few things in London and, if that went well, they would then see if there was merit in going down to the research station where some of the software was being prepared. After that, Martin had said 'with any luck, we should be able to get you on a train back to Wales the same night'.

When he was shown into the Minister for School's room at the Department for Education, he was introduced to

Professor Jamieson, who had been the lead Survey Officer. As he listened intently to the discussion the other two were having, it became apparent that there was going to be some kind of trial for what seemed to be a new approach to pupil behaviour. Something different had been touched on at the earlier meeting in Bristol, and it now looked as if they were going to run with it. Most of it was too technical for Bryn to fully understand, never mind contribute to. It was only when they got down to the topics of how to manage a trial that he became interested.

'We're hoping this is the part that you can help us with Bryn' Martin said.

'I'll be only too happy to give you advice on anything you want' Bryn replied.

'No, actually, it's not so much advice as practical support we are looking for.'

'What do you think I can do?'

'We've discussed what we need to do to make an assessment of any new procedures statistically valid. Professor Jamieson here feels that we need to trial our new approach in at least two different geographical areas, to make sure that we get a broad enough base and avoid getting too narrow a set of results. We need to make sure we get these procedures right to avoid others refusing to accept the results. At the same time, we need to do the research trial in at least one area where the current situation is not good. That way we have a chance of showing a marked improvement in behaviour – if our views are borne out by the results. We want to make your area one of the areas used. How do you feel about that? I'm happy to talk to your Chief Executive on the Council, if you feel it might help to smooth the way?'

Bryn was pleased that he had obviously been heard when he spoke at the previous meeting. Who knows, he thought, where that may eventually lead to in terms of his own involvement with politicians here in Westminster. He was sure he could handle any objections that appeared at the local Council level, but he recognised that as much support as possible at the Chief Executive level could only help to smooth things when they got down to discussing the practicalities of any trial. He said 'I'm certain our Chief Officer would welcome a phone call from the Minister' as he smiled at Martin.

Martin continued 'Professor Jamieson and I intended to go down to the Research Station this afternoon for a short meeting with the scientists involved in the software associated with this method. We understand that it is very nearly ready to be operational. There have been some difficulties in tying down some of the more difficult bits of the communications end of the system, but as I understand from the Head of Station down there, they seem to be nearly ready to trial it out. As you're here today, and you will be involved in managing the introduction of the trial in South Wales, we thought it might be a good idea for you to tag along and see a bit of that end of the business before heading back home. Is that OK with you?' Bryn enthusiastically nodded his agreement.

* * * *

Peter had tried to get in to see Arnold as soon as he arrived at work the next morning, but it seemed Arnold was going to be very busy on other matters right up until lunch. His secretary was able to say 'he has a meeting booked in with some people who are coming down from London at 1430. I was going to ring you anyway, because he has said he would like you there too.' Peter knew he would not be able to advance those timings. He would just have to bide his time.

42.

PETER WAS SHOWN into Arnold's office at 14.30 prompt. Almost immediately, he asked Arnold what was going on in relation to his research.

'I'm not sure what you mean by 'going on' Peter,' he replied. 'Production of the hardware is coming on stream nicely and from what I've heard your software glitches seem to be all resolved, aren't they?'

'Pretty much. What I'm more concerned with now is how this is going to be used. I was not happy at the thought that a piece of Research designed to alleviate the symptoms of disease, should become the basis for controlling the movement of criminals and now also possibly terrorists – or should I say potential terrorists?'

'But Peter' Arnold said in his most condescending tone 'you must see that there are very real benefits to society as a whole from both of these uses, surely? I shouldn't have to explain the real benefits of being able to trace those who have shown themselves to be in total disregard of society's accepted norms of behaviour. If, as now seems likely to be the case, we are able to modify their behaviour wirelessly, then that is also a good thing, isn't it? In those circumstances, we may be able to help both the individuals regain their place in our society without lengthy and expensive incarceration, either in prisons or in hospital. In any case – and I think we've covered this ground before in one of our previous chats – we are straying into areas which are more the responsibility of our political masters than ourselves as scientists, aren't we.'

Peter was just about to respond, when there was a knock at the door and Arnold's secretary showed his three visitors in. She said she would bring coffee in a few minutes while they were getting themselves settled. As a result everyone was looking at her as she left. None of them saw the look of amazement on Peter's face when he saw that the second of the two men entering the room was Bryn, his father. His mind raced back to the conversation he had only the day before with his mother Sally, and then the Sunday lunchtime revelations from Sandra Wilson. It was all true!

Bryn was equally astonished.

'What in God's name are you doing here?' he asked.

'I work here dad, and have done for the last two years.'

'Well I'm damned' Bryn went on

Peter's response of 'you probably will be' was lost in the hubbub of the rest of them making their own introductions.

Arnold had caught some of the words between Peter and Bryn and said in astonishment 'you two know each other?'

'You could say that' Peter responded. 'Bryn here is my father. I haven't seen him for a little while and I had no idea he was moving in these circles.' He was on guard when he saw the look on Bryn's face. He had felt he was delivering something of an insult, but Bryn clearly saw it as a compliment.

Arnold was oblivious to the interplay. 'That might help matters along then' he said. 'I want to use this meeting to put some flesh onto the bones of an idea from our Minister Martin Cook' – he nodded across to the Minister. 'None of you will need reminding of the results of Professor Jamieson's survey into pupil behaviour.' He looked questioningly at the rest of them. 'Well then, the idea is that we should trial the effectiveness of this new approach in a couple of disparate Geographical areas and then assess it as a tool for wider use across the Scholastic world.' Peter looked as if he was about to explode, but Arnold frowned him down and continued 'It has been decided that we should choose two areas where the recent survey showed most need of improvement. One of these is a suburb of the Liverpool conurbation and the other is the Gwent area in South Wales. Mr Bryn Thomas is here in his capacity as the Chairman of the Education Committee on the County Council there.'

Professor Jamieson said 'Bryn and I have had time for a short discussion on the way down, and I'm pleased to say that he is all in favour of the trial taking place in his area. I believe that Martin Cook will also be talking to the Chief Executive of the Gwent County Council with a view to giving them any assistance we can from the centre to make sure the trial is conducted without fuss. This help will include a substantial additional grant to Council funds for them to dispense as they see fit.'

Peter just couldn't hold back, although he knew the reaction it would generate in the others.

'You mean you intend to bribe the local area into going along with this idea?'

There was a general intake of breath at that remark, but Martin Cook came in smoothly.

'I think that is stretching the truth just a bit, don't you Peter?' he said. 'Setting up a trial like this is over and above what we normally expect from the area. As we are the ones who are asking for that extra effort, it must surely be right that we ensure that there are sufficient funds available to make sure it is run properly. Bryn has explained that, as usual when any changes to a system are being introduced there will be some Councillors who will be unhappy. As he has also said, however, providing additional funds to the area like this will more than likely be enough to bring on board any otherwise wary Councillors.'

Bryn continued by saying 'of course it would be too big a trial to have every child in the area involved. That's why we more or less agreed as we were coming here that the most sensible way to approach things would be if we concentrated what are still limited resources on those children where we may see the biggest improvement. We – all schools – keep registers of occasions when incidents of unacceptable behaviour take place. The idea would be to limit these trial procedures to those children on that register. Once we see the benefits we expect as part of the trial to become apparent, we will be able to roll out the programme very quickly.'

Peter was getting whiter by the minute. He eventually could take it no longer. 'I have to raise the most serious objections to this idea' he said. 'I had no concept that my research might be used in such a way. It is to my mind an immoral use of the work I have done, and might well breach Civil Rights Legislation in several areas.'

The others all looked at each other. Martin Cook again moved in.

'Peter, why do I get the feeling that you don't like us all very much? Peter slowly looked over at the Minister and said

'Is that now an additional requirement of the job, Minister?' There was an embarrassed silence.

Bryn started to say 'now look here Peter...', but he got no further. Peter spun around to him. 'No, just for once in your life, it is time for you to 'look here'. This is an approach I cannot and will not condone. For God's sake father, are you actually prepared to allow this to be done to your own grandchildren? Have you lost all sense of perspective? Or did you just never have any?' Peter realised that he was becoming so agitated that he was in danger of losing the others. Then he also realised that he didn't care whether he did or not. He had probably never had them on his side anyway, had he? He just knew that he had to speak out and speak out now. Whatever the consequences, if he didn't, he would never be able to look at himself in the mirror again.

'If you all cannot see how grotesque this approach to children is becoming, then there seems little point in continuing this discussion, with me at least. I don't know what agenda you are all following – he looked pointedly at Arnold – but it is not one that I can or ever will subscribe to.'

He rose and left the room.

There was stunned silence for a moment and then Bryn said 'he always was the wilful one in the family, the one who always had to get his own way, otherwise the toys came out of the pram. If the software you were talking about earlier is now up and running, or nearly so, do we really need him from now on?'

Professor Jamieson said

'I'll get back to you Bryn when I've assembled all the pieces we need for the trial shall I? Martin Cook, who had been fairly silent after Peter's departure, turned to Arnold and said

'I know it's not strictly within my direct responsibility, but perhaps Arnold here needs to speak to Peter again. And fairly soon I think.'

They all nodded.

43.

AFTER PETER HAD left the meeting, it didn't take him long to clear his desk. He then got into his car and went straight home. He needed time to think. When Rhona arrived at her usual time, he was still in a raging mood. She had never seen him quite like this before and it took her some time to get him to even sit down rather than storm around their lounge.

When he did, she had to sit in amazement as he explained about the meeting. She felt much the same as he did, in fact she said at one point that she would probably have walked out too if it had happened at her place. None of that helped Peter. 'We are talking about a Minister of the Government here, not some kind of loony. We are also talking about my father, who has finally shown exactly what family mean to him. Absolutely nothing'.

Gradually the rage diminished. It was replaced by something much colder – a determination to do something. The question was, what?

* * * *

Gareth was seething. He knew he had always been the one to keep cool, keep a lid on family disagreements. He had felt it just made for a better life for all of them. After all, he had reasoned with Maddie on more than one occasion, you only get one chance at life, what was wrong with trying to do it as gently as possible?

Maddie hadn't always seen it like that. They had agreed to disagree on several occasions when she had felt he needed to take a firmer stance. As Gareth reflected on some of those as he drove in to the Garage on Wednesday morning, he realised with some surprise, that those occasions had always been something to do with his father. Maddie, he smiled ruefully to himself, wouldn't have been surprised.

As he pulled into the forecourt, he knew that today was going to be different. He didn't know where it would all end, but as he had sat back last night after explaining to Maddie what Peter had told him in that late night phone call, he realised that this was one fight he couldn't afford to lose. Maddie had made it clear that his whole marriage might depend on these next few minutes and hours.

* * * *

'THEY'RE WHAT?' Donald McLeod roared at Colin.

'I said, Donald, that Rhona has just come off the phone to say that they are going ahead with this experiment to try and modify the behaviour of children. Apparently one of the areas earmarked for the 'trial' is Gwent where Peter's brother Gareth and his family live.

Peter has gone off to speak to his brother, and is apparently talking about resigning his position in research as a result of that decision.'

'They must be mad' Donald said.

'That may be so, although I think they have just lost any idea of what is regarded as acceptable behaviour from our elected representatives. The question, though, Donald is what, if anything we can do about it? Rhona asked if we could come up with anything that might help.'

* * * *

Gareth was switching off his engine when the phone rang. It was Maddie, and he could hear from her voice that she was clearly quite agitated.

'Gareth are you there yet?' she asked.

'I've only just arrived' he said.

'Is Bryn there?' she asked.

'I don't see any sign of his car, but I can't see from here if the garage door is open yet, why?' he asked.

'I passed Mrs Wilson – Sandra – on my way into school this morning. I told her about Peter's phone call last night, and she wasn't surprised. Apparently one of the Education Department's managers has already been on the phone to all the Schools in the area asking them to send in the register they have of all examples of bad behaviour. They say they want to know the names of the pupils involved for a trial they will shortly be making.'

'I suppose something like that was inevitable once they decided to have a trial in this area' Gareth replied.'

Maddie became even more agitated.

'Gareth, you still don't see it, do you?' she said.

'See what? Gareth replied.

'Remember that little incident recently with Mr Jones? Gareth, our Nathan's name is on that list.'

Gareth went quite cold.

263

44.

'THERE COULD BE some positive advantages that might come out of all this, Colin' Donald said when they had agreed that they would do whatever they could to help – even if it was only on a temporary basis. 'If Gareth and his wife are prepared to come and visit us here, it would at least get them out of the way for a couple of weeks and give them, and us, a chance to think about what else might be possible.'

'I think that's a really good idea for starters.' Colin replied, 'but we must be careful to provide help in any way we can as long as it is something they want, and not press our views on them. The last thing they will need right now is for someone – anyone – to be putting unwanted advice their way.

'I think though' Colin continued, 'that we need to concentrate right now on how, and how quickly, we can get them up here and away from what I can envisage as being an unholy mess down there for some time to come.'

'It sounds as if you have some ideas about that' Donald said.

'Yes I do actually' Colin went on.

'Rhona was telling me when we spoke on the phone that Gareth and Gordon Morrison had hit it off quite well when we were all having that meal on the Sunday afternoon.

Apparently they have already said that they would like to get together and give the two boys the chance to go out on Gordon's boat sometime soon. I wondered if a phone call from me to Gareth might change those plans a little.'

'Why don't you do that then' Donald said 'it would still be something of a big step for them to get away for a holiday in the timescale we might be looking at. Maybe Rhona should be talking to Gordon at the same time and then let them see if the two of them can reach a satisfactory arrangement.'

'Actually' Colin said, ' I've been thinking about how we – you and I – can provide some help of a practical nature that might help things along'.

'Tell me what you had in mind, then. Don't keep an old man waiting.'

Even as he said it, Colin could see a smile beginning to play across his older brother's face. Was it possible, he thought, that for once, just for once, they were, as the old saying went, about to sing from the same Hymn sheet? Surely not. Then he remembered how Donald had been after the Sunday meal.

'Mum has been all alone since dad died, rattling around in that big house of theirs. I know you've moved in with her, but I didn't see that as a permanent arrangement for either of you. Even if it were, you are out a lot of the time on church business. I was initially thinking that it would be the perfect place to put Gareth and his brood up if and when they came here for a holiday. Mum would welcome the company from Maddie and we would all love to have

Samantha running around under our feet for a little while, wouldn't we?'

By this time Donald's face was a picture. His smile was getting bigger by the minute. 'Now that's what I call a really good idea, little brother.' Colin could hardly believe his ears. The big gruff man standing in front of him hadn't called him that in years.

'You can count me in on this one Colin' Donald said as they solemnly shook hands and smiled at one another.

'I'll speak to Rhona and then Gareth as soon as I can then – big brother.'

45.

As GARETH TURNED the corner of the unit housing Valley Mobile Mechanics, he saw Peter standing at the door waiting for him.

'What the Hell are you doing here?' he demanded.

'I couldn't sleep after our talk last night, so I decided to come down here and have my say' Peter responded.

'You must have left damned early to be here at this hour' Gareth said.

'Well, there are some things you just have to do, if you care enough, aren't there?' Peter said as they both went inside.

It was only a few minutes later that they heard the distinctive engine note of Bryn Thomas's latest four wheeled acquisition. As he walked into the main office of the building, he was startled to see both his sons there.

'What brings you down here?' he said to Peter.

'Do you honestly not know Father?' Peter said. 'Are you really so far removed from the real world that you have no idea why I might want to talk to Gareth here about our last conversation?

'Now listen here' Bryn started to say, but was interrupted by Gareth.

Speaking very calmly and quietly, so quietly that Peter

had to strain to make some of the words out, Gareth said

'No father, I think it's about time for me to talk and you to listen. You know, or you should do, that I've always tried to keep the peace in the family. I was always the one who kept quiet when the rows were raging between you and Mum. Even when you said the most outrageous things to her. I always tried to find excuses for those outbursts. I always wanted to believe that you were working under some strain that we didn't know about. Do you remember the occasion when you told Mum that she had killed YOUR daughter? I don't suppose you even remember saying that, but it was something no one else will ever forget – or forgive. It never occurred to you that the baby would have been her daughter and our little sister too, did it?

I was always the one who kept quiet whenever you let rip after deciding that either Peter or I had not done exactly what *YOU* wanted and when *YOU* wanted it. It didn't seem to matter what either Mum, or Peter or I felt or wanted, far less needed. No, the only thing that mattered. The only thing that has ever mattered to you, was that everyone you came into contact with did what you wanted. You've only ever had three priorities in your life, haven't you? Bryn, Bryn and Bryn.

I see now that what I saw as an attempt to cut short all the arguments, you saw as a weakness. You've gone through life assuming that the only voice that mattered was yours. I suppose I'm a bit to blame for that. If I'd spoken out sooner, maybe we could all have had a meaningful relationship. But I didn't, and we don't.

I know we all have to live in the world we have, rather than the one we would like it to be, but it is still sad to find that someone we all wanted to care for should care so little for us.'

Bryn tried to interject, but Gareth held up his hand to silence him. Peter was amazed. No, it was more than that, he was in awe of his elder brother's calmness. It was so different to the way he had shot his own mouth off in that recent meeting and, he realised, so much the more powerful because of the calmness which Gareth maintained.

'No father, I've said I'm talking and even if it might be just for this once in your life, you will listen, or you can leave. The choice is yours.'

Bryn Thomas was having difficulty recognising this man standing in front of him. If the truth were known, he was having difficulty recognising the man as his own son. In other circumstances, he might have been proud of his elder son taking centre stage like this, but not when he was on the receiving end.

'As far as you're concerned, all this is merely another attempt to control everything and everybody you come into contact with, isn't it? It's not really about improving standards in our schools or even saving money on Psychiatrists trying to help the most vulnerable children in our society. For you, it's all about control – just like everything else you've ever done in your life. Mum left when she couldn't take it any more, Peter left when he couldn't take it any more. If it had been up to Maddie, there is a better than even chance we might have left too, but I still wanted to try and have a relationship with my father.'

'The news this morning from Maddie has finally shown me how stupid I was to still care.'

'What news?' Bryn managed to get in.

'The news that you are so far removed from reality that you are prepared to allow your own grandson to be injected in some crazy plan you have to improve his behaviour.'

'I didn't agree to anything like that' Bryn protested.

'Oh yes you have. Nathan was accused, quite wrongly, of 'setting up cheek' to one of the teachers in his school recently. As a result his name is now on the offenders register – an offenders register that has had to be passed to the Education Department as one of those children who should be subjected to this trial of yours. Maddie and I decided when it happened not to make waves over the issue. It was, we felt, a bit of a storm in a teacup and so we decided to let it go, even though we knew Nathan had done nothing wrong.

If we had known that this plan was being hatched, we might – no we would – have had a lot more to say. That was mentioned the last time Peter here came down to visit, remember? All you had to say then was that the area needed a shaking up, and you were just the man to do it.'

'It's the same story all over again, isn't it father?' Peter said quietly in an unconscious emulation of his elder brother's approach. 'As long as you're being seen to be 'in charge', anyone else, even those who should mean something to you, is of no consequence.'

'There is no point in saying anything more father is there?' Gareth said 'you are far too old to change your ways, and at long last I've realised that. Just like the rest of the family, I'm not prepared to take it any more.

I'll get James, our Company Solicitor, to draw up the legal documents dissolving the Company as soon as he can. I will fulfil the commitments we have to our existing customers, but will take on no more business. The Company is effectively closed for business as of now.'

'And what will you do, if you carry out that threat?' Bryn roused himself enough to say. 'You're far too young to retire, and there is precious little extra business around this neck of the woods if you try to start up as a new company.'

'To be honest, I don't really know as yet.' Gareth replied. 'We have been invited to visit Rhona's relations up in Stornoway at any time for a holiday. Maddie wants to do that, and I think I do too. It will give us time to think.'

As the brothers walked out of the building, Gareth turned back to Bryn, tossed him the garage keys, and said 'lock up will you? And you can keep the keys, I won't be needing them again.'

46.

RACHEL JONES WAS working hard cleaning up in the kitchen of their Hotel. It wasn't often they were able to set aside time like this, but there was a window of opportunity before the next influx of guests who were scheduled to arrive at the weekend. Even then, there were only three rooms that were going to be used. She had said to Gordon earlier that morning that she might be able to give him a few days off! This season had been very hard for them both. Long hours stretching from six in the morning to make sure breakfasts were available from seven, through evening meals and then working behind the bar until gone midnight had left them feeling as if they were out on their feet most of the time. Thankfully the busy season was fairly short, and they were now moving into 'walkers and ramblers' times when everyone wanted to move at a slower pace.

It was all worthwhile when some of the smaller guests had left calling her Auntie Rach. That had happened on a few occasions and she was surprised at the way she felt about it. Maybe it was hormones that were talking to her, but she had already decided that she was going to have a serious talk about the future, their future, to Gordon, when things quietened down.

When the phone rang, she hoped Gordon might be near enough to answer it. The words 'I'm cleaning the drains outside darling' shouted through the open window showed her that wasn't going to happen. As she dried her hands, and went over to the phone, she thought it would be another booking. Ah well, that was why they bought the place to start with wasn't it?

'Hello Rachel. Is Gordon by any chance around?' She recognised Rhona's voice and said 'he's up to his eyes in drain fluid right now'. Rhona was about to say she would call back, but Rachel went on ' we've both been hard at it since early morning. If you give him a minute to wipe the dirt off his hands I'm sure he would like a break.' Rhona said, 'it might take a while for this call' and Rachel said 'in that case I'll need to get him a cup of coffee while you chat.'

By the time the coffee was put down in front of him, Gordon was looking very serious indeed. He wasn't saying much, which presumably meant, thought Rachel, that Rhona had a lot to tell him. Eventually he said 'leave it with me, Rhona will you? I've got Gareth's number. We were going to arrange a date for me to take him and the boys out on the boat. I guess we need to finalise those arrangements pretty quickly. I'll get back to you soonest.'

As he put the phone down, Rachel said 'I can see that something is up, perhaps you'd better tell me what it is eh?

* * * *

Peter had driven over to Gareth's house right behind him after the meeting with Bryn at the garage. As they went up to the front door, Maddie opened it.

'Did you see him?' she asked.

'Yes' Gareth replied.

'And?' she said.

'Perhaps we should talk about it inside rather than here on the doorstep, eh?'

Samantha burst past Maddie when she saw Peter coming up the path. 'Uncle Peter, is Auntie Rhona here too?'

'No sweetheart' he said 'she is still at home. She had one or two things to do. She will be coming over to see you all very soon though.'

'Oh good' Samantha said as she took his hand and went in.

As they all walked into the lounge, the phone rang. Maddie answered and then turned with a puzzled face.

'It's Colin, Rhona's uncle from Stornoway. He wants to talk to you Gareth.' Gareth took the phone as Peter said 'I'll take the women into the kitchen and tell Maddie what happened earlier, while you're on the phone.' Gareth acknowledged with a wave of his hand.

Peter had almost finished bringing Maddie up to speed on the earlier conversation with Bryn, when they heard Gareth say 'Thanks for the offer, Colin. I'll get back to you as soon as I can sort things out at this end and make some plans. We'll speak again soon.' The three of them moved back into the lounge, and Gareth said to Maddie 'I think you had better sit down.'

47.

AFTER GARETH HAD explained to Maddie and Peter what Colin and Donald McLeod were offering by way of holiday accommodation, he looked at his wife. 'What do you think we should do for the best?' he said. 'I know we're not supposed to take the boys out of school for a holiday, but this looks like it's too good an offer to turn down, don't you think?'

Maddie smiled and said 'why don't I get on the phone to Mrs Wilson right now and tell her that we are doing just that as soon as we can make travel arrangements? If the Education Department want to make something of it, I for one would love the chance to talk to the South Wales Argus about what is going on under their noses right now. In any case, if they operate to their usual level of competence, we'll have gone, and might even be back again, before they even notice we're not around.'

She walked over to the phone and was about to pick it up when it rang. 'Maddie?' came a voice she seemed to recognise.

'Yes' she said.

'It's Gordon Morrison here, you remember we met with Rhona McLeod and her two uncles recently?'

'Oh, hello Gordon' she said, which caused both Gareth and Peter to look up at her.

'Is Gareth there?

'Yes, and so is Peter.'

'Can I have a word?'

She handed the phone over to Gareth.

* * * *

Peter's mind was working almost as fast as his engine as he drove back down the M4. Gordon's suggestion that instead of taking the boys out for an afternoon run on his boat, he should take a couple of weeks off from his hotel business in Barmouth and run the whole Thomas family up to Stornoway had been taken up with alacrity by Gareth and Maddie. Luckily, he thought, Gordon Morrison didn't have any weddings booked for his boat for a few weeks, otherwise the arrangements which they had now put in place would have been quite different.

Finding a land route for Gareth and his family to get up to Stornoway for a holiday would not have been easy, nor cheap. They had mulled over how the return trip would take place, and when. Maddie had called a halt to the indecision on that by saying that they would cross that bridge when they were up there. A bit like Rhona, she displayed common sense which sometimes eluded the men on issues like that. 'The important issue right now is getting the boys – Nathan in particular – well away from Gwent Education Authority' she had said, and of course she was right.

As he had left Gareth, they were about to phone Mrs Wilson at the school and let her know that Daniel and Nathan would not be in class for around two weeks. Maddie had said she would do the necessary. After the conversation they had all had at the hotel, she didn't envisage too much by way of argument from the Teacher. If she got any, that would just be too bad. She was emphatically not going to ask for permission, no matter what the rules said.

Now that the difficulties at this end of the world looked like being resolved, at least temporarily, he could begin to think more clearly what he needed to do himself. For that he needed to speak to Rhona.

* * * *

Beyond Tomorrow

48.

WHEN GEOFFREY WILLIAMSON rang the doorbell at the entrance to the flat he knew Peter Thomas shared with his girlfriend, he wondered what he would find. He didn't even know if Peter would be there. No one at the Research Station had seen or heard from Peter since he had walked out of the meeting some days ago. Everyone was agog to find out what had happened though. There had been a lot of talk about what might or might not have happened, some of it quite lurid. Scientists were just as curious about personal 'flare ups' as they were about their own scientific experiments.

He wouldn't normally have done this. But Arnold had almost pleaded with him to find out what was happening with Peter, and anyway, he liked Peter. After his own experiences with politicians and SPPS he, more than perhaps anyone else, had some idea of what Peter must be feeling right now.

Peter was surprised to find Geoffrey on his doorstep. He and Rhona had agreed last night that he had to go back in to the Research Station, even if it were only to hand his security pass in. Rhona had said at one point

'Are you absolutely sure this is what you want to do? Remember the conversation you had with Gareth when you had decided that you needed to stay and at least try to keep some kind of control over things like this.'

'Yes, I remember all too well that talk we had. What has changed is the knowledge now that I will not be able to make any difference at all to what the politicians want to do. Even Arnold was not prepared to fight my corner. When you get no support, even from those who should be on your side, then the writing is on the wall, isn't it?'

Rhona didn't have an answer to that, and she knew better than to try when Peter was in that kind of mood. As she left a little earlier she had just said 'keep calm, Peter. Shooting your mouth off will not change anything either.'

'I know.'

* * * *

Now that Geoffrey was standing there, Peter felt the bile rising in his throat again, and that was with someone who was on his side! Keep calm, he said to himself. Remember how Gareth had spoken to their father.

Sitting down in the lounge, Geoffrey said 'I'm sorry things have developed like this for you Peter. Arnold asked me to come, I suspect because he didn't know how you might react to find him on your doorstep. I think he wanted to keep himself above all this if he can.'

'Is that a little chink of reality breaking in there Geoffrey?' Peter replied. 'Does no one who attended that meeting see the grotesqueness of what they are planning? Do none of them recognise what it would all mean out there in the real world that we all live in?'

'Arnold did say that he felt, as most of us scientists do, of course, that we seek the truth in our experimentation. We examine how things work and try and see ways in which we can make them work better. He also feels, and this is where I move away from his thinking, is that how the science is then developed, is more a matter of the needs of the society we live in, not the exclusive preserve of what he calls 'the select few'. I nevertheless have some idea of how you are feeling, Peter. Remember it happened to me with the developments in my SPPS system? We went from animals out on the hills to Army rescue action without anyone asking what I thought.

Science has always operated like this, hasn't it? Once it was proved that the Earth was not the centre of the universe, all sorts of theories became fashionable. Some, perhaps even most, were crackpot, but others opened up avenues of further research until we are where we are now. My development of SPPS had nothing to do with terrorists or criminals. Others took the idea and went down those other routes with it.'

Peter had been thinking about this kind of discussion for some time, since he had left South Wales. He knew that he would have to have it with someone, sometime and somewhere. Speaking quite calmly and quietly he replied.

'No Geoffrey. I know you mean well, but what is happening here is nothing like your experiences. Oh, I know it was about changing the direction of your Research as this is, but this time it is very different, isn't it? This time we are not talking about keeping track of the criminal element in our society, we are talking about *CHILDREN* for God's sake!'

'My Research was aimed at helping sick people to have some kind of quality of life. These changes are now trying to control the most vulnerable and the most innocent people in our society. They're not sick, they're merely learning how to behave as they grow up. Some of them have problems, yes, but they're nearly always problems which we as a society have created.

These are the very people we should be doing our utmost to protect. Instead we are trying to control them. And for what reason? Because some politicians feel that it would make life easier for the rest of us! My God Geoffrey, what kind of society are we becoming when we hand over the raising of our children to people whose first thoughts are 'why do we spend money and effort trying to help with their problems when we can just put an implant into them – because it makes life easier for us! Easier to manage them, easier to control them!'

Geoffrey knew there was no answer to that, at least not one he could either think of, or would be happy to put forward. He raised his head slowly and said 'what are you going to do about it?'

'Frankly, as of this moment, I don't know. What I do know is that I am not coming back to the station. I cannot put my name to anything like this, and I'm not going to let anyone try. If I came back, I would be doing exactly that.

I've already been offered a couple of jobs in the States and I might take one of those up. Gareth and I have already had that conversation and I don't like the idea of my work being corrupted in the way it is now happening.'

'When you decide, will you let me know?'

'I'll try.'

49.

PETER AND GARETH had been on the phone to one another several times since Gareth and his family had arrived in Stornoway. The trip up had been uneventful. The whole family had been excited when they arrived in Barmouth and the excitement continued for the three children all the way north. The weather was calm and the seas were, for that part of the world, surprisingly smooth. Maddie acted as cook and bottle washer for them all. It had taken four days and on one night, as Maddie snuggled into Gareth while Gordon and the other crewman took the night shift, she said 'this is idyllic. It really is. If Stornoway is half as nice as this trip is becoming, we are going to have a fabulous time.'

While Gareth agreed whole heartedly with those sentiments, he wondered what the future in South Wales might hold for them on their return. When he voiced those concerns, Maddie was quick to cuddle even closer and said 'let's worry about that nearer the time and not spoil the whole two weeks'. He turned and gave her a kiss, but his mind was racing.

* * * *

Gareth knew that he would shortly have to talk to Gordon Morrison about the arrangements for the return trip. Gordon had gone off as soon as they all arrived, to spend time with his father. He had said he would come around in a few days time to sort those details out. They had now been here for just over a week, and so 'those few days' Gareth knew, were coming to an end. They would bring with them the need for a decision that he had been mulling over. He had to talk to Maddie first, of course, but it might also be a good idea to talk to the McLeod's before that, and get a feel for their views.

Donald and Colin were to be found most evenings in the hall adjoining their Church. As Gareth went in through the front door, he still hadn't fully thought through what he wanted to say but, he reasoned, if he got a negative set of vibes from them, he wouldn't need to think any further than he had already.

It was Donald who looked up first as he heard the footsteps on the wooden flooring.

'Hello Gareth. What brings you here? Have you come to join our congregation?'

That was already becoming a standard joke between them. As soon as the family had shaken the dust off their feet, Donald had asked if they were coming to the Sunday service at the Church. Gareth was not particularly religious, but he knew that Maddie felt the need to attend on a regular basis. Maddie had immediately taken the brothers up on the offer, but Gareth had respectfully declined.

'Not yet, Donald' he said. What I was hoping to find was some help in coming to a big decision on my family's future.'

The two McLeods looked at one another.

'Fire away then Gareth' Colin said.

* * * *

After Gareth had finished explaining the way he was now feeling, he stopped and said 'have you got any views on such a move? It is a huge step for us to make, and I can't afford to get it wrong, both for Maddie's sake and even more so because of the children. It is after all their future I am talking about more than anything else, isn't it?'

'Yes, of course it is' Colin said. 'Donald and I had already talked about just this possibility. We cannot and would not try to make such a decision for you, but perhaps if we run through some of our thoughts, it might help you reach your own decision on what is best for your family.'

Donald went on 'We both know how difficult it is to get good mechanics to stay around on the island once they get qualified. There is a lot more money to be made working for one of the big franchises in Inverness, or even Fort William. Nearly everyone disappears – and who can blame them. The bright lights and the big money has always been an attraction for many of our people. The result is that there is always a shortage of people around with your skills.'

'So you think there is a possibility of there being enough work here to allow me to make a reasonable living for my family?'

Both Brothers nodded vigorously.

Colin continued 'We feel you and your family would be a real asset to the community from several points of view. Apart from your own work skills, Maddie has shown in the last few days that she is someone who would fit in here on the social side very well indeed. On top of that, her skills in the school situation would mean that she would quickly become a valuable member of the local community. The children are well mannered and polite. All in all, as a family unit, you would be made very welcome if you should decide to make the move a permanent one.

I think that the only question which you need to resolve is whether you and Maddie are sufficiently disenchanted with what is happening down south to make such a move on a permanent basis. What I do know is that both of us would do everything we could to help make it happen.' He looked across at Donald and saw him smiling broadly. 'All children, as you have heard me say several times before, will be happy wherever they are, as long as they are with Mum and Dad, and as long as Mum and Dad are happy.'

'I guess' Gareth said 'that my next move has to be to speak to Maddie about this. I don't think I'll get much opposition! Then I suppose I'll have to talk to Peter and explain what is now on the agenda.'

'Speaking of Agenda's' Colin said. 'What is Peter doing

about things at his end? The last time we spoke, you said he was determined to do something about all this, but wasn't sure what might have any effect.'

'That's right' Gareth said. 'None of this is really public knowledge yet, and he's afraid that by the time it does come out into the open, it will all have started and then it will be too late to stop. When we were on the phone last night, I asked him that very question. All he could say was 'God knows'. He stopped 'I'm sorry, I should have remembered you are loathe to be seen to take the Lords name in vain.'

Donald said 'don't worry about it. In the circumstances, No-one would consider that the case'. He looked across to Colin to seek a response there, and saw his brother's face light up.

'What is it?'

'I've just had an idea.'

'Are you going to tell us, or keep us in the dark, then?'

'I've just thought of someone who might be seen to be talking in God's name, or at least with God's authority behind him. Perhaps even more importantly, he is in a position where he might be able to talk to people who can stop this thing in its tracks.'

* * * *

When the three of them split up a little while later, they each had a job to do before they went to bed:

Gareth was going to talk to Maddie, although he knew that wouldn't take long, and then phone Peter.

Donald was going to speak to Rhona after talking to Gordon Morrison.

Colin, on the other hand, was going to speak to the man he had met at the recent Conference in Wales. He felt that the discussion he was about to have with The Bishop of Winchester, would be the most important phone call he was ever likely to make.

50.

Peter Thomas wondered what they did in the world before phones, particularly mobile phones, came into being. He had spent a long time on the phone last night to Gareth while Donald had been talking to Rhona. He couldn't say he was terribly surprised at Gareth's news. He knew from his long association with Rhona that there was an affinity between the Scots and the Welsh that had been in place since the first Celts took over. It had since been fostered by a common antipathy towards the 'Arrogant English'.

He had tried hard not to see things like that, after all he knew a few arrogant Welshmen! This latest development fitted the same set of ideas though, and he was sure his brother would settle in quickly to the family's new surroundings. When he had told Rhona, she had merely said ' there is no doubt our big day will have to be in Stornoway after all then, eh?'

He sighed as the phone rang again, demanding his attention.

'Peter?' came the voice of Colin McLeod.

'Yes' he said.

'Can you do me a big favour?'

'If I can. It's not as if I'm very busy at work anymore.'

'Can you pick me up at Heathrow – the flight from Glasgow is scheduled to land at 13.40 tomorrow? Most of the flights down south from Glasgow go to Stansted, but I thought that was quite a long way to ask you to come and get me. I've booked in to a hotel not far from you – it's called the Alton House Hotel – as I've arranged a meeting (they called it an audience would you believe?) the next day with a friend of mine who lives not very far from you – the Bishop of Winchester.'

'Not a problem, I know the hotel well. I suppose it would help if I took you down to Winchester to see this man? It's no trouble for me, and it would be a lot easier for you, I imagine. I was arranging to take my Mum out for the day. She lives close by here too, so I might bring her along, if you don't mind.'

'That would be a great help thanks. It would be nice to meet her anyway.'

* * * *

On the road back from Heathrow the next day, Peter suggested that perhaps Colin might like to go out for a meal that evening. Rhona had suggested it, and it would be an opportunity to relax with Sally Thomas and get to know some more of the steadily extending family. Colin jumped at the idea. A lonely meal in the South of England had not been his first choice for a nice evening. Peter explained that

Walter, his Mum's partner, was away on business and so couldn't join them, but he would bring the two women with him before they went to The Hen and Chicken – a country pub/restaurant set on the roadside between Alton and Farnham. 'Nothing too pretentious, you realise' Peter had said 'but it serves good food at reasonable prices.'

'Sounds ideal' was Colin's reply.

* * * *

Gareth and Maddie were finishing breakfast on what was, for them, the first day of a new life. They knew they had to start making plans for all sorts of issues, but Maddie had not slept for much of the night, her mind racing with all that needed to be done. She was so excited, she could hardly get the meal finished quickly enough. She would take Samantha with her as well as the two boys to sort out the formalities for getting them registered for school and also with Doctors. She didn't know how long that might take, but she did know she had to start soon. The two boys in particular were now, in her mind, no longer on holiday.

Gareth was detailed off to go to the council offices and see what rented properties were on the local market, and when any might be available. He was opening the door as Gordon Morrison reached up to press the outside doorbell.

As Gareth started to speak, Gordon held his hand up. 'It's OK Gareth' he said. 'Donald has already given me your news. I was coming to sort out the details of the trip back down south, but I guess we don't need to bother now, eh?'

'No Gordon, at least that's what we hope will be the outcome. Maddie is trying to sort the kids out right now with schools and Doctors. I've got to talk to the Council about housing, and then set about finding work. I'm accustomed to running my own business, but I know that part of the package is likely to be me finding work somewhere – anywhere – to start with. If I have to start at the bottom again and work my way up, that will still be better than the problems that are going to emerge in Wales when these plans finally become public knowledge.'

'How about me helping you with both of those issues?' Gordon said. 'I can run you over to the Council offices, and wait for you. But before I do that, I should take you for a run up the harbour side and see what we can see there.'

'How would that be a help?' Gareth asked.

'Just wait and see.' Gordon replied.

Fifteen minutes later Gordon pulled the car that he'd borrowed from his father off the main road, partway up the Brayhead beside the weir where the River Creed disgorged itself into Stornoway harbour. The Marina where Gordon's boat was moored was only a couple of hundred yards further downstream. Gareth looked out of the front passenger's window and said

'It's very pretty here. What has this to do with helping with my efforts to move to Stornoway, though?'

'Gordon smiled and said 'take a look out of the car behind

292

and to your left. Across the street.'

When Gareth did so, he couldn't see anything at first. Then he noticed a gap in the row of terraced houses which fronted onto the river. The white finished building at the edge of the gap proclaimed itself to be 'Celtic Clothing Kiltmakers and Outfitters'. Higher up there was another sign. It said 'McLeod's Garage' with an arrow pointing up into the gap. Splashed across that was an even bigger sign which said FOR SALE. He turned back to Gordon, who said 'it's been up for sale for quite some time, according to dad. The owner is retiring and doesn't have anyone in the family who can take it over.'

Gareth sat with his mouth open, until Gordon said 'why don't we go over and take a little look?'

51.

ALTHOUGH THE SUBJECTS discussed had not been pleasant, it had nevertheless been a good evening Colin McLeod thought as Peter had dropped him off at his hotel last night. Meeting Sally Thomas had also proved to be enlightening. She had also met the Bishop once before and said that he seemed a sensible sort of individual who would react as they hoped at the message they were about to give him. It was, however, Rhona who had suggested that, as each of the others had a different angle to the situation, it might help the Bishop to see the whole picture better if they all went in to see him. As she had said 'a mother, a scientist and a churchman – almost a full house of opinions.'

The Bishop was pleased to see Colin again, and was also pleased to see Sally. He remembered her from the meeting in Alton. When he was introduced to Peter, he looked again at Colin and said 'I hope this isn't going to be too high-brow for a scientific simpleton such as myself?'

Colin laughed and said 'I think if I can understand what we are about to discuss, you will have no problem whatsoever, My Lord.' The Bishop replied 'please Colin, let's not stand on ceremony here. For the purposes of this meeting I am Walter. Nothing more, nothing less. Elsewhere is elsewhere.'

The others looked at one another and Peter thought maybe, just maybe, we have an individual here who is able to see the world without rose tinted spectacles.

It took nearly two hours. The three of them could see the changing emotions on Walter's face as they went through their story. It went from outright incredulity to barely suppressed anger. In the middle of it, the Bishop's secretary came in to remind him he had another appointment scheduled for that afternoon. He stopped asking the others questions for a minute and then said 'send my apologies, I will not be able to make it today. Tell them that something extremely urgent has come up. Oh, and while you're at it, find out if the Prime Minister is at Chequers this weekend or if he is out on his travels. If he is there, tell him I would welcome a few minutes of his valuable time.'

They were saying their goodbyes at the door a little later when the secretary again made an appearance. 'The Prime Minister would be glad to see you at mid-day on the Sunday, if that would suit.' she said.

'Tell him that would be suitable' he replied then, turning to the three of them, he smiled and said 'I think the 'cool' thing to say now is 'watch this space.'

* * * *

Gareth, in the end, had had a mixed day. The Council said they would look at the possibilities, but they could not give him anything like a timescale off the cuff. They had a stock of houses, but they were in the middle of a large improvement process where tenants were being decanted into available properties while their own were being refurbished. They would try and find something suitable, but it might take some time.

The Garage looked like it was possible though. Gordon had taken him to the agents who were selling the property and after a short discussion he came away feeling he could make it work. Timing was going to be crucial here too. He had a rough idea of how much he would be entitled to from the dissolution of the business in Wales, and he thought that might be enough to get the one here. He didn't know however, when the monies might become available, and as the Stornoway business had been on the market for a while, the current owners would jump at any other offer if it came in before he could get his money together.

He had only started to explain the position to Maddie when Donald McLeod came into the lounge. 'How did it all go today then?' he asked.

Maddie said 'why don't you join us. Gareth was just starting to tell me.'

When Gareth had finished, Maddie said 'so we haven't really made much progress, have we? Schools are OK, they will take the boys no problem, all I need to give the school to start that ball rolling is give them an address where they can contact us. But we need to have the rest in place too and we won't know about these other things, including an address, for some while, it seems.'

Donald meanwhile had been thinking. These people were his kind of people. Honest trustworthy, sensible and as for Samantha! He knew it was nonsense, but he was beginning to see them all, and her in particular, as the family he wished he had. He looked over at the two young adults trying to make a new life for themselves, and knew he would – had to – do anything he could to help.

'Can I interrupt both of you?' he said.

'Of course Donald. Forgive me, we were too wrapped up in our own problems to even remember you were there.'

'Well, from where I'm sitting, I don't see much of a problem.' They both looked at him in astonishment.

'As I see it, there is a simple solution to them both.

One. You are currently in residence here. I need to talk to Mum, of course, but I don't see any reason why this current arrangement cannot continue for the foreseeable future. That, at the very least, lets you sort out the schooling issue doesn't it? All you then need to do is inform the school authorities of a change of address for the children when you sort yourselves out properly.

Two. You want to make an offer on this garage?'

'Yes.'

'I can loan you the amount you've said you need until the money comes through from Wales. When it does, you give it back. No interest. We don't do that to families, at least not up here.'

'Wait a minute Donald' Gareth said. 'We don't put people

into that kind of position.'

'No, Gareth, you wait a minute. Can I trust you to repay the money as soon as you are able?'

'Yes of course.'

'Then the subject is closed.'

The three of them stood and hugged in the middle of the room.

52.

IT HAD NOT been a pleasant meeting for either of them. Frank Sutherland could see the tension in the Bishop of Winchester's face even as he had welcomed him into his study at Chequers. It didn't get any more pleasant as he listened in silence to what he was being told. At the end, the two men just looked at one another. Before Frank could get his thoughts in gear enough to say anything, the Bishop said

'Unfortunately, Prime Minister, I have to ask you just one question. Were you aware of these plans?'

The Prime Minister said 'would it make any difference?'

'Only in a small way' the Bishop replied.

'What is that?' Frank said.

'Your answer to that question will dictate whose name I quote when I speak to the papers and television channels later this week. I like to be sure of all my facts when I talk to the communications industry. I think we both know the likely outcomes once the press are made aware of what has been going on – both for the individuals involved, and also for the ruling party under whose watch these things were being planned. And rest assured they are going to be made aware.'

Frank Sutherland knew – he had said it often enough himself – that any fool can keep a good ship running smoothly. It is when things go wrong that you are really tested, and sometimes found wanting. As the Prime Minister, he knew that he would not be forgiven if he was ever found wanting.

He cursed silently to himself as he realised that he had not 'kept his eye on the ball'. He knew the potential that Hilary carried with her. He had seen her in action too many times not to know. No matter how many times he had said to himself 'well done' as she sorted out some problem or other, he had also said 'not again' as she had done her own thing. As he looked up at the Bishop, to find him looking intently back, he realised that these were excuses, not reasons, and they would be seen as such by the man opposite.

He straightened himself. This was one situation he couldn't afford to get wrong. At the end of the day, it was either her career or his, and that, he knew, was no contest.

He needed time however.

'Can you give me forty-eight hours to try and put things right on this? he asked.

'I will not make those appointments with the press until after Tuesday, if that would help' the Bishop replied. 'But I will wait no longer than that Prime Minister – and I would urge you not just to try. This is one time you must succeed.'

As he waved the Bishop goodbye a few minutes later, Frank Sutherland turned to his private secretary and said 'Contact the Cabinet Secretary and the Home Secretary. I want them both in No10 tomorrow at eight o'clock – and that is a.m, not p.m.'

* * * *

Gareth Thomas wanted to speak to Peter and tell him about the decision he had reached and what they were now planning. First, though, he had another phone call to make.

Bryn Thomas's first words when he heard Gareth's voice were 'oh, it's you. I thought it might be Peter phoning to apologise for the mess he's landed me with down here. I thought it was all going to happen as I had planned, but no, I gather he's muttered in a few ears and it's all getting stopped. I've had to unpick all the plans we were working on and it's made me look foolish in the process.'

As Bryn vented his anger, any last vestiges of sympathy Gareth had for his father drifted away.

'Anyway' Bryn continued, 'what is it you want? Changed your mind about the business have you?'

'No Dad' Gareth said. 'I thought it was right that I should let you know that we – all of us – are staying up here. Maddie likes it, the kids love it, and I know I can make a good living here too.'

There was a silence from the other end of the phone and then Bryn said 'and what about me?'

'I wondered how long it would take you to get back to your favourite subject' Gareth said. 'You've got your Golden

Labrador, I'm sure he will be only too happy to be controlled. Maybe you'll care for him a bit more than you cared for the rest of us, but I won't be holding my breath.'

Gareth hung up and walked out into the sunshine to play with Samantha.

Epilogue

Three Years Later

Peter Thomas and his wife, Rhona are now happily bringing up their two year old daughter, Sally, in America. They moved to Massachusetts after Peter decided to take up an offer from the Massachusetts Institute of Technology (MIT) to continue his more recent research into Schizophrenia and other personality disorders. Sally Thomas attended their wedding, held in the Free Church of Scotland on Kenneth Street in Stornoway, and Samantha was a bridesmaid. Bryn Thomas did not attend.

Following her resignation from Parliament, Hilary Watson was turned down for several high profile Legal partnerships in the City. She is now working for a firm in Aldershot offering legal aid to soldiers who have been alleged to commit atrocities while on active duty in Afghanistan and elsewhere.

Colin McLeod continues to work at the Nicolson where he is now Head Teacher of Addison House – the house for Gaelic speakers. He and Gareth Thomas take Nathan and Daniel out on his boat at every available opportunity.

Gareth Thomas and his wife Madeleine are highly respected members of the Stornoway community. Madeleine is working as a special needs assistant at Stornoway Primary

School and is well regarded for her efforts to help children at an early age overcome learning difficulties. Gareth has developed a reputation for high quality work at reasonable costs, and is currently in negotiation with the Airports Authority about the possibility of opening a service facility at the airport. Gareth speaks to Peter on the phone each week without fail, and he and Madeleine are planning a visit to America next year.

The two boys have settled into Island life well. Nathan is beginning to show real talent on the rugby field, and is already talking about helping Gareth when he is older. Daniel is never far from the science laboratory and wants to be like 'Uncle Peter'.

Donald McLeod suffered a severe heart attack almost twelve months ago. He is making a slow, but steady recovery and is visited almost every day by Madeleine and Samantha. He hopes to go back to work with the Town Council shortly. He has arranged a meeting in the near future with William Russell, his solicitor, to discuss his will. While he has not settled all the details of that in his mind, he is already certain that Samantha Thomas is going to be a very rich young lady in due course.

Gordon Morrison's father was taken ill some time ago, and has now been diagnosed with MS. Gordon and Rachel are close to deciding that Barmouth is unlikely to ever be the once hoped for gold mine, and are considering his father's offer of a partnership in the Stornoway hotel he still manages. Rachel is still waiting on the proposal of marriage.

Frank Sutherland left Parliament after the Conservative Party lost the General Election heavily last year. He still travels into the City regularly from his home in Surrey to attend board meetings of the three Companies where he is now a Non-Executive Director.

Martin Cook also left Parliament and is now employed as a finance manager at a local charity based near his home in Canterbury. He has lost all contact with Hilary Watson.

Sally Thomas still lives with Walter Hughes at their home in Hampshire, but no longer does occasional work for Hilary. She has two holidays a year – one to Stornoway and one to America where she can still see, and spoil, and spend time with, her grandchildren.

The Bishop of Winchester has not had any more interviews with the national press, but is concentrating his efforts in bringing the faiths closer together. He also maintains his interest in youth work.

Deniz Mehmet is now on the payroll of MI6. He is working 'somewhere' in the Middle East. He hopes that the implant he had recently asked to be installed at the base of his neck will be sufficient to enable him to be found and then laid to rest beside his family, when the time comes.

Bryn Thomas was not re-selected by his Constituents at the last Local Election. He now spends his time walking his dog in the Sirhowy valley, and drinking in The Castle Inn – his local pub in the village of Pontywain.

Alone.

THE SECRET IN THE WOODS

The English who live in the far south east of the country have an unshakeable belief in the absolute certainty and rightness of their own personal views. Jimmy Tasker, the newest appointment to the rank of Detective Constable in the Metropolitan Police, was aware of that when he moved into the small market town of Alton in the north of Hampshire, shortly after his wedding to Jean his childhood sweetheart. He was, however, not so aware of the multitude of criminal acts that were considered acceptable to the local population, based on these often widely differing beliefs.

Moving on detached duty into the anti-terrorist section of the Met, he was soon to find out.

As he was faced with this miasma of conflicting attitudes and actions, he discovered that it could all backfire too easily on his beloved Jean. In the end he was forced to consider, for the first time, whether his decision to become a policeman had been the right one.

THE CANCER OF CORRUPTION

Jimmy Tasker was an officer who didn't suffer fools gladly. His time in the Metropolitan Police had brought him up against a few already. Now in 1975, he knew that his tour of duty in the anti-terror unit was coming to an end and he expected to be moving on. He didn't expect that move to mean leaving the south of England.

Asked to investigate the possibility of a 'mole' in the South Wales Police, he soon wondered if he could uncover the truth – before he made enemies of most of the senior officers he dealt with.

Tragedy on a personal level had to be dealt with alongside trying to unravel a far reaching web of deceit and lies which eventually led him back to the higher echelons in the Met.

SUFFER THE LITTLE CHILDREN

Jimmy Tasker would admit that some of his progress through the ranks of the Metropolitan Police, was due to him being in the right place at the right time. A senior officer had once told him that 'it's often better being lucky, than being clever'. As he looked at the sodden bundle which had been a six week old baby, before being fished out of the water on the French coast, he felt neither lucky nor clever.

When he saw the look on his wife's face, he knew that he would do anything and go anywhere to bring those responsible to justice. That determination would take him across Europe and uncover a web of crime that was almost unimaginable to the ordinary man in the street.

In the process, he would be faced with a personal decision that would have far reaching consequences for his marriage.

AS DREAMS DIE

When Jimmy moved with his wife Jean back to the South of England, they were both anticipating a new and pleasant chapter in their lives unfolding. While there were no guarantees, they knew that there was at least the possibility of them being able to adopt a baby – something that South Wales could not offer.

What Jimmy did not anticipate, was becoming embroiled in the intrigue and violence surrounding political changes in a Government far away from England's shores. He anticipated even less the damaging and long-term effects these changes would have on his family.

THE FINAL SOLUTION

Jean Tasker had known from the outset that Jimmy was destined for great things in the police force. The death of their daughter Heather had knocked them both sideways, and she was determined that her illness would not cause him any further grief.

Jimmy wanted to be with her during that period, but a request for help from his old friend Walter Carter, meant that was not going to happen. Travelling to Barking every day to help their manpower situation, was not easy, but he had never been able to turn down a request for help from 'real coppers'.

Dealing with a double murder which had its origins in the Second World War, gave Jimmy and his new colleagues difficulties he could never have imagined.

In the end, they managed to resolve these in time to prevent yet another murder, but not in time for Jimmy to say goodbye.

THE DARK SIDE OF PARADISE

When his beloved wife Jean died, and his sister Annie came to look after him, Jimmy Tasker knew that his whole world was slowly changing around him.

He was ready to throw himself totally into his work as a DCI in the Met, until the 'offer' of early retirement appeared out of the blue. They needed an answer, and he needed a break. While he was laying on the sand in Barbados, things were happening back in London that would shape that answer and send him on a quest which would uncover the 'other' side of the Caribbean paradise.

It would also show him another future – if he cared to grasp it.

ABOUT THE AUTHOR

Ian Lumley is a retired Civil Servant. Having spent most of his working life in the Personnel function of a variety of Government Departments explaining rules and regulations to others, he decided after retiring to venture into more creative writing areas. He has had some twenty poems published in the first two years of beginning to write.

Although a fervent Scot, he lives with his wife in South Wales, where his grandsons take up most of his time when he is not writing for pleasure.

His previous works also include some thirty short stories and a series of six novels detailing the career of a Scottish (what else?) detective and his wife transplanted to other parts of the United Kingdom. If you would like to read more of his work, he can be contacted through his website at:

www.ianlumley.co.uk

Lightning Source UK Ltd.
Milton Keynes UK
UKOW01f1953220917
309708UK00005B/251/P